chapter one

On Christmas Eve 1914 a German 'Taube' aeroplane was sighted over Sheerness and on the following day seven British seaplanes attacked the German naval base at Cuxhaven. But in the Sussex village of Becket's Hill, the first Christmas of the war was little different from any other year.

Late in the afternoon, Molly Farmer decided to take a walk, and her son Alan settled down at the kitchen table to write a letter to the War Office, requesting to be trained as a pilot in the Royal Flying Corps. He wrote the letter three times, and, finally satisfied with the third attempt, carefully burned the others in case his mother found them.

Taking down the copy of *The Theory of Flight* from the bookshelf in his bedroom, he removed Colonel Starke's letter of recommendation from its hiding place between the pages. There was absolutely no need to feel guilty, he told himself as he put both letters in the envelope and sealed it. It was highly unlikely that he would be accepted for training, so it was pointless worrying his mother unnecessarily.

*

That same afternoon, carols were being sung in a base hospital in Northern France. Reminded of village Christmases long ago, spent with his father and his brother, Will, Harry Farmer sat listening in his wheelchair, dwelling sadly upon the loss of his pocket watch. The watch had been shattered in the incident in which Harry had lost his left arm. If only he had kept the watch in his right-hand breast pocket instead of the left-hand one ... such a shame! The pocket watch had originally belonged to Harry's father, had been handed down to his elder son, Will, and Harry had acquired it on attending Will's funeral in the June of 1912.

It was still hard to believe that Will was dead, Harry mused, as the orderlies came around with the tea and a little parcel for each man – they had gone to a lot of trouble, bless their hearts.

'You'll soon get the hang of doing things with one hand,' the orderly said as he unwrapped Harry's parcel. 'There you are! An ounce o' tobacco.' And he winked. 'We saw you had a pipe there. Come on! I'll wheel you outside and we'll have a smoke up.'

Muffled in a blanket against the keen December air, Harry learned to strike his first match with one hand, and, as he sat there smoking peacefully, the sudden flutter of wings in a nearby coppice took him back eighteen years to an April afternoon when he and Will had gone out shooting with Molly. How she had screamed at the very first flutter; clutching Will's arm as he pressed the trigger, and watching with relief and joy as the partridge flew safely on. How strange Harry had thought the girl then. How he had shaken his head in despair at his brother for marrying such a contrary-minded creature, and what a dance she had led them both when she first came to live in the house. But looking back on it, who could blame the poor girl? Leaving her comfortable life in the town to keep house for two brothers who scraped a bare living in a country smithy and whose sole experience of the feminine touch was their plain old Aunt Nell who smoked a clay pipe on the sly, and came in only twice a week just to do the washing and bake enough bread to last them until her next visit.

They had first seen Molly Grayson on that long-promised holiday in Brighton, soon after their father had died, and three weeks later Will had brought her home to see the house. She had stood at the back door, a golden-curled doll, giggling away as Harry rushed upstairs to change out of his dirty smithy clothes.

Five months later she entered the house with a wedding ring, a determined little smile, and a pair of dainty but capable hands that immediately set about cleaning up a house that had 'lain fallow in accumulating grime' since Harry's mother had died when he was born. And a woman around the house was to be a startling new experience for seventeen-year-old Harry.

WINGS

THE BBC TELEVISION SERIES

Cast

Alan Farmer	Tim Woodward
Molly Farmer	Anne Kristen
Harry Farmer	John Hallam
Lorna Collins	Sarah Porter
Tom Chater	Reg Lye
Charles Gaylion	Michael Cochrane
Captain Triggers	Nicholas Jones

Writers
Barry Thomas, Arden Winch, Julian Bond

Directors
Donald McWhinnie, Jim Goddard,
Gareth Davies, Desmond Davis

Series created by Barry Thomas
Produced by Peter Cregeen

Barry Thomas has been writing for television for twenty years and was Script Editor for the very successful series, *The Onedin Line*. He once adapted Gogol's *The Government Inspector* for comedian Tony Hancock, collaborated with Francis Durbridge on the marathon eighteen-part thriller, *The World of Tim Frazer*, adapted *How Green Was My Valley* for live transmission from the Cardiff studio, and has been Script Editor and writer for *Dr Finlay's Casebook* and *Z Cars*. In spite of a fair bit of experience he is still naïve enough to marvel at the work of directors and actors who do the real job of getting the shows on the screen.

He is the creator of the television series, *Wings*. He was a navigator in the RAF, and for a short time – not short enough! – he was a parachute jumping instructor. This gave him a taste for insecurity and so he became a writer. Born in Barry, Glamorganshire, he now lives in Walton-on-Thames with his wife, Connie, and their five children, and has no time for hobbies.

WINGS

Barry Thomas

Pan Original Pan Books and the
British Broadcasting Corporation

First published 1977 by Pan Books Ltd,
Cavaye Place, London SW10 9PG,
and the British Broadcasting Corporation,
35 Marylebone High Street, London W1M 4AA
© Barry Thomas 1977
ISBN 0 330 25043 4 (Pan)
ISBN 0 563 17169 3 (BBC)
Printed and bound in Great Britain by
Cox & Wyman Ltd, London, Reading and Fakenham

On the morning after she arrived, Harry dashed in from the smithy to fetch a small file from the toolbox under his bed, fell over her on the dark stairway and avoided knocking over her pail of water only just in time. She was breathing heavily from her exertions, her pretty little face all anger under the springing curls. It had taken her an hour and a half of town-bred thoroughness to scrub away the metal dust ingrained by years of lazy men thumping up and down the stairs in disgusting country boots; and for the next week or so she looked sharply down at his feet whenever he came in at the back door until he acquired the habit of taking off his boots and padding about the house in a civilized manner.

During her second week, having accustomed herself to her new surroundings and resigned herself to the prices in the four small shops (where, in her opinion, there was not nearly enough competition), she began to take an interest in the work of the smithy. It began one morning when one of Richards's big shires was brought into the yard for shoeing. Molly stood at the back door watching Tom at work, fitting and nailing the shoes. Crusty-tempered, the angry heat of years spent at the forge emanating from his reddened, deeply lined face, Tom Chater had started work as a boy of twelve, pumping the bellows for Will's and Harry's grandfather. Although Will Farmer, as owner, was rightfully the smith, Tom considered himself the kingpin of the smithy and battled Will's authority with a sharp tongue backed by the skill and knowledge of forty years' experience. Since Molly's arrival at the house, Tom had treated the 'new missus' with cautious respect; suspicious of her charm, perturbed by the directness of her gaze, ashamed of his lustful feelings whenever she passed the front window of his cottage on her way to the shops, and secretly indignant at Will's proud insistence that his new wife was not just milk and roses but a town woman with a mind of her own. Tom did not believe in women having minds at all, still less minds of their own.

Molly asked about the nails he was using, and Tom stressed their importance. Any old nails would not do at all. They had to be hard yet not brittle; specially shaped to hold fast for a good depth and made of a metal that would wear at the same rate as the shoe.

'Otherwise the poor beast would very soon be standing on six nail points,' he said, with a little smile at her dainty feet as they tripped over to the nailbox. 'And if you tried that, missus, you'd find it most uncomfortable, I daresay.'

She examined one of the nails and Tom explained the purpose of the special shaping. The wedge-shaped head had to be exactly made to allow for the expansion in driving the nail home, not only to make it fit, but to be perfectly adapted to the hole 'pritchelled' for the nail. Molly was intrigued by the delicate operation of the pritchelling and amazed that it could be accomplished by such a rough-looking tool.

'Even we country people have our delicacies,' Tom smiled, with a sly wink at Harry, who was Tom's 'doorman' when he was shoeing. 'You're very interested in that nail, missus.'

Yes, she was. She wanted to know where the nails were made, and on learning that they were forged by skilled specialists in Sweden and the North of England, she looked astutely at the box of nails, enquired the cost of such a box, raised her eyebrows at the answer, and wondered if the smithy might not be more profitably employed in forging the nails rather than merely hammering them into hooves.

Tom's kindly, helpful manner vanished abruptly. Harry, sensing trouble, sniffed and looked towards the back door as if something might be burning in the kitchen. But Molly was oblivious.

'There must be a decent profit in these nails if so few people are making them.'

'No doubt there is,' Tom growled. 'But there's more to life than profit, missus.'

Fortunately, at that moment Will came out of the smithy, and seeing his wife's interest in the proceedings, told Tom to take a breather; he would finish off the shoeing of the shire himself. Tom looked darkly at him and grumbled into the smithy, pausing at the doorway to remind Will that this one could be a bit 'tetchy' with its hindlegs.

Will smiled the remark away, already rolling up his sleeves

to display his muscular arms to full effect before his wife, pleased that at last she was taking an interest in his trade. Not that she had spoken disparagingly of it; but she had given him the impression that she considered the veriest dolt of a townsman could pick it up in an evening or two.

'Harry's still learning the trade, of course,' Will said loftily. And with something of the aplomb of a circus ringmaster, he took the farrier's toolbox and placed it just behind the shire. 'He's acting as doorman for the time being. An assistant you might call him in the town, I suppose.'

Molly looked enquiringly at Harry, who dropped the pliers and politely explained that it was his job to receive the horses, bring them into the yard, have a good look at them to see how they stood, usually remove the old shoes, and fetch and carry for the smith. Molly nodded in a way that suggested he might have been better employed in doing something useful.

'There's a lot more to being a good doorman than you might think,' Will said. His smile was loving and his tone gently reproving, like a father instructing an adored but wanton child.

Tom now reappeared in the smithy doorway with Ted Pearce sidling after him. Ted, the smithy carpenter, with a face the colour of putty and clothes that were much too large for his thin body, had decided to join Tom in 'watching the new missus watching'. Any excuse was good enough to draw them out into the spring sunshine. The dark warmth of the smithy, cosily welcome in the winter months, stifling and oppressive in summer, was simply an atmosphere to avoid as much as possible in the spring. And the sunshine was good for Ted Pearce's cough, which had kept him awake at nights for close on eighteen months. The apprentice joined them, but from force of habit, stood a little apart. He was referred to as 'young 'un', never by his name; that was an honour reserved for the time when he had earned his farrier's certificate. But inexperienced as he was, he had already learned not to stand within arms' reach of the men. However good-humoured the prevailing mood, he knew all too well how suddenly the wind could change. With four men and a boy working together day in and day out, tempers could quickly flare over the most trivial difference of opinion, and the 'young 'un' would always get the clout that settled the matter. If someone as much as turned to him to pass the time of day, the poor lad's arm would rise instinctively in a gesture of defence.

'Oh, it's easy enough just to remove an old shoe,' Will said, stepping beneath the shire's rump and lifting the hoof on to his thick, hard thigh, with a purred 'up, my beauty'. 'Not so easy to remove it without causing damage.'

And he demonstrated the use of the hand-anvil and hammer to cut off the clinched ends of the nails. Then he took the pliers from Harry, and with swift, deft movements, lifted the shoe at the heel, tapped it back, drew the exposed nails and pulled the old shoe off. 'Look at that lot,' he said, as he proceeded to remove the dirt and clean the sole with a knife. Then he cast an experienced eye over it for possible defects. 'There! That one's ready for the new shoe.'

Molly, now aware of the two men and the boy standing in the doorway, smiled across at them. They gave a little shuffle and smiled pleasurably back, enjoying the sunshine and hoping that the demonstration would last until dinnertime at least. Will, seeing Molly's smile and spurred to further efforts to impress her, displayed the full extent of his skill with a speed and flamboyance that sent the shire's belly shuddering.

'There, there, my beauty,' Will said, patting its rump consolingly. Harry had now come up with the two new shoes and Will told Molly to watch carefully and she would learn a thing or two. 'Every horse has its little peculiarities, you see. You get to know them all in time—'

The shire snorted, shook its mane and turned its head sharply, causing Molly to step back in alarm and knock the box of nails over. As the nails scattered about the yard, the trio in the doorway turned quickly away to stare into the darkness of the smithy until the grins had left their faces, then turned back again, looking solemnly on as Harry helped Molly to pick up the nails.

'Careful what you're doing with those nails,' Will said, trying to keep the irritation out of his voice. 'They cost, you know.'

Molly quite agreed. And lost no time in putting forward her proposal once again.

'What? Us make shoeing nails?' Will exclaimed. 'We couldn't do that.'

Molly couldn't see why not. Will explained that it was not their business to make shoeing nails. They were shoeing and general smiths.

'I'd have thought "general" might have included the making of the nails,' she said. 'And there's a good profit, I'm thinking, from the price on this box.' And she looked at Tom, who had underestimated the price by fourpence. 'There's not much special about them as far as I can see. Apart from the price.'

'You know nothing about such matters,' Will said, ruffled now. The time and trouble taken in forging the nails would cost them more than buying them. 'Weren't you seeing to the dinner?'

'I didn't mean making them just for our own use,' Molly said. 'I meant making them wholesale.'

Will was aghast. What the hell was she talking about? The watching trio now decided to ignore the sunshine in favour of the fun that was to come and moved to watch in undetected comfort from the darkness of the smithy.

'My family have been blacksmiths here for four generations,' Will said, unable to keep the quiver of emotion out of his voice. 'And you want our son to be a nail-maker?'

'How do you know he wouldn't thank us for it?' she asked. And she gave a little sniff in Harry's direction. 'He might want something more from life than standing about with pinchers in his hands.'

Will snatched the shoe from Harry.

'Bring me those bloody nails,' he muttered. 'And it's not as simple as that. It's every man to his own trade, you know.'

She threw the nails at his feet. The shire snorted and shook its mane.

'And who said anything about us having sons?' she said. 'Taking a lot for granted, aren't you?'

'Don't talk soft, now,' Will said, conscientiously lowering

his voice. 'There was no point in us getting married if you don't bear me sons.'

'I see!' she cried. 'So that's why you took me away from the comfort of my home, is it? Apart from making a drudge of me in that dirty old house.'

'Be quiet, girl!' Will hissed, darting anxious glances about him.

'All you want from me is the fifth generation,' she cried, even louder. 'And a son of yours might well think four generations under a horse's behind quite long enough.'

Will hammered the nail and the shire struck out in reply. Molly shrieked as Will sprawled with a howl on the stones of the yard.

'There, there, my beauty,' Harry said, anxiously consoling the shire and glaring at the men who were diving into the smithy with their hands pressed over their mouths.

'My God!' said Molly, helpless with laughter. 'That was one little peculiarity you didn't know about.'

In the smithy, Ted Pearce sank on to the bench, both hands pressed on his chest, wheezing that he shouldn't laugh any more or he'd start his cough going.

'Married a fortnight,' grinned Tom. 'If that shire had been an inch or two to the left, they'd have had to call it a day, I reckon.'

'Perhaps she'll put some liniment on it for him,' the apprentice grinned up at them. And got a clout round the ear for being too young.

That night, lying in bed in the next room to the newly married pair, Harry heard Will scolding Molly for laughing at him in front of the men. She giggled and made a comment Harry couldn't hear. Will made it clear to her that he was 'the smith and the owner' and so needed the men's respect. Harry then heard his own name mentioned, and Will saying that Harry was entitled to earn his living in the smithy but that Will, as the elder brother, was the owner. That was the way it always had been and the way it was now. And then, as if to erase any impression of covetousness he might have given her, Will added, with a rather stoic yawn, that he bore the sole responsibility for the place. Molly readily agreed that it was a heavy burden for him to bear and suggested that he should lay it down for both their sakes, sell up, and open a business in Lewes. There was a long silence. Then Will reminded her that she had wanted to come and live in the country. No, she hadn't, Molly retorted, she'd been dragged there, much against her will, and she proceeded to complain about the trees. This puzzled Will. It puzzled Harry, too, and he sat up in bed and pressed his ear to the wall to try and hear her reply. But she must have had her head under the clothes, he reckoned. Then he heard Will reminding Molly how much she had loved the trees on the day she arrived; she had said that she'd always loved trees and that they were the one delight that had made up for all her apprehensions about other aspects of living in the country.

Harry remembered the fuss she had made when she had seen two labourers beating a walnut tree with hedge-bills until the sap ran freely. She had spoken sharply to the men and before they could explain what they were doing, she had gone off in a huff saying how cruel it was and that one day the trees would be revenged upon them all. Will had run after her to tell her that the beating was done to make the tree more fertile; then he had winked and said he would be taking a stick to bed with him that night. She had smiled despite her anger, dug her elbow into his ribs, and said: 'You'll pay for it, all the same. You mark my words.'

Harry was naturally curious to know why she had changed her mind about the trees. After a mumbled argument Will decided to cut the trees down. That was wicked, she said, and went off on a tirade against country people who had no appreciation of the beauties they had been blessed with. Very well, Will answered, he would simply cut off the branches that were tapping against the window on windy nights. There was not much wickedness in that, surely, and anyway, it was worth a bit of wickedness if it meant getting a good night's sleep. This led her on to ask why they always had to go to bed so early. Country folk needed their sleep, Will told her. They worked hard. And early to bed, early to rise, etcetera; to which she replied that it hadn't done much for the pockets or the wisdom of the people she had met so far in Becket's Hill, who all hated her because she came from the town and dressed herself respectably instead of going about in old clothes that smelled like rotting apples. And it wasn't the tapping of the branches that worried her. The trees made the room so dark. And the room overlooked the yard, so that she couldn't open the window because of the fumes from the smithy fire. He knew very well how she loved fresh air. What was the point of coming to live in the country if she couldn't breathe the air? And anyway – Harry's room was bigger. She had measured them both that afternoon!

The next morning, Molly watched the arrival of the cart from the wood-yard in Caxton.

'Seven miles? Is that the nearest timber merchant?'

Ted Pearce, who always checked the consignment and helped the carter to carry it in, assured her that it was, whilst Tom and Harry exchanged meaning glances. It looked as if they were moving on from nail-making into the timber trade.

'What's this wood called?'

'Ash!' Ted wheezed.

'Why is there so much of it?'

Ted explained that his work as a smithy carpenter was chiefly concerned with wheels, cart shafts, tool handles, and agricultural implements made and repaired in the smithy, and that ash was the best wood to use because it was as tough as oak and would not splinter. Quite often, of course, Ted made other things to order that were not in any way concerned with work done in the smithy. What sort of things? came the immediate response.

'Wheelbarrows! Harvest ladders! Now they are made from ash. They need to be curved, you see, so the ash pole is split down the middle so's you can bend it. Again, as it's a wood that won't splinter, the ladder can be pushed off a stack without fear of it breaking.'

Molly nodded and looked thoughtfully at an old cartwheel

that had been lying about in the yard for two years or more. According to Will, since the felloes were split there was no possible further use for it, though the spokes still seemed good.

When Ted had told her the uses of all the other woods, their merits and weaknesses, the difference between sawn and riven timber, and explained at great length that the use of cheaper woods was dearer in the long run, Molly seemed perfectly satisfied and called Tom, Harry and the 'young 'un' to give Ted a hand to carry in the load. Reluctantly they moved off to do her bidding. Ted seemed concerned.

'Oh, I shouldn't drag them away from their work. Me and the carter can manage this lot.'

The carter, in fact, had done little so far but give Molly black looks and frown at his watch.

'You can't manage it on your own,' she panted, setting down an oak post against the bench. 'And you ought to do something about that cough, you know.'

'Oh, but I am,' Ted said, grave-faced. And he nodded his head towards the far end of the shop. Molly's face paled when she saw the coffin. Then Ted laughed. 'Joking, that's all. No, it's not for me. Not quite yet, eh?'

And he tapped the coffin with his toe. 'Elm, that is. Very good against the damp. Special order for Granny May in Leadby Street. Suffered with the rheumatics for years.'

Molly smiled uneasily. Then she saw the stick. It was hanging from a rafter with a heavy stone tied to its end. The top of the stick was bent over the rafter with wet moss placed above it. It was a walking-stick, Ted told her. He was making it for his father. The stick was an ash sapling. Oh yes, they were plentiful enough, and mostly found in thorn hedges.

'Now there's a thought,' Molly remarked. 'We could make them by the dozen and get someone to sell them for us in Caxton market. I'll mention it to Will.'

Ted made no comment but from his expression he was not too keen on the notion of turning his shop into a walking-stick factory.

'That's the last of it,' Tom said, sullen-faced, and dropped the ash poles on the floor, dangerously close to Molly's feet.

15

'Careful,' Harry said. Tom glared at him and stamped into the smithy. Harry told Molly she wouldn't be very popular for a while.

'I know,' she said, with a sharp little sigh. 'Every man to his own trade. And mine will be making pegs soon by the look of that tin.'

Ted Pearce was paying the carter from it. And when he returned the tin to its home in the kitchen drawer there was exactly sevenpence ha'penny left in it.

The 'tin' had been a bone of contention between Molly and Will ever since the day she had arrived. Will told her that the tin had been kept in the drawer since his grandfather's time, and long before that, very likely. All payments for work done in the smithy were put into the tin. The weekly wages for Tom and Ted Pearce, the bills for coal, iron, wood and other materials required for the smithy, were all paid directly from the tin. How Molly's father ran his drapery business in Lewes was no concern of Will's. No accounts were kept here; there was no need for them. One knew exactly where one stood simply by looking in the tin. 'How do I pay the bills when there's no money in it?' Molly had asked. There were no bills for her to pay, Will had told her. Just her bits of shopping. And the shops would wait for their money. No one ever made a fuss. Now and then, when the tin contained a reasonable amount – when you could jiggle your finger and not see the bottom, he had grinned – one of them would buy a shirt or a pair of socks, and Will would go to The Plough on a Friday evening as well as a Saturday. And he had laughed and kissed her on the cheek. Oh yes, she could have a new blouse or a frock whenever she wanted, so there was no need to look so concerned. 'I quite understand that you've never had to worry about money in the past, my love. And you've no need to start worrying your pretty little head about it now. Just leave all the money worries to me. I'm used to them.'

A blacksmith's life in Becket's Hill was a precarious one. Most of the time Will and Harry were dependent upon the vegetables in the small garden. And on occasion, during a hard winter, their stomachs were as empty as the tin in the drawer, and they often went to work in the smithy without any breakfast. As Will's father had been fond of saying: 'A blacksmith works to oblige, and he's lucky if he makes a living as well.'

'Well, I'm not here to oblige,' Molly had snapped, when Will quoted this at her, 'I'm here as your wife.' And she didn't care how many generations had dipped into the tin and shrugged their shoulders when it was empty, its proper place was on the back of the fire. The family's financial system was primitive. They behaved like cavemen around a communal chunk of meat, which even outsiders could come in and have a tear at.

'Tom is not an outsider,' Will had shouted. 'He's been working for us since he was twelve years old. He gets the coal cheaper. That's why we always leave the paying to him. Just as we leave Ted Pearce to pay for the wood. He understands the prices. And he's as honest as the day is long. He wouldn't help himself to a ha'penny from that tin.'

And he reminded her that she had come there to learn their country ways, not to infest their simple life with the tight-fisted complications of the town. He couldn't see that they would be any better off with an account book. Writing down tuppence in a book would hardly make it fourpence in the tin! And that was that. He would hear no more of it.

On the morning that the wood had been delivered, Will was down at Collins's farm repairing a new reaping machine that had been made by a 'mechanical genius' in Caxton. He returned just before dinnertime and called in at the smithy to see 'how things were coming along' before going into the house. Having had a hot and irritating morning with a piece of machinery that should have been wrapped around its inventor's neck, he was in an even darker mood after talking with Tom and Ted Pearce.

Molly was ladling from a pot on the range when he came in from the wash-house – and he stood there, trying to keep his eyes off the tin which had been placed beside the cruet, with the sevenpence ha'penny lined up along the bottom like a poor little army.

'I've just had words with Tom and Ted Pearce,' Will said.

'And in future I must ask you not to interfere in the business of the smithy – or of the carpenter's shop.'

Molly appeared not to have heard. She remarked that there was broth and bread for dinner. What they would do for tea was another matter.

'You had better ask that tin,' she added. 'Wash your hands before it gets cold.'

'We are blacksmiths here,' Will said, harshly. 'And blacksmiths we will remain. Not nail-makers! Or walking-stick makers, either.'

Harry dribbled the spoonful of broth down his chin.

'Walking-stick makers?'

'You keep out of this,' Will snapped. 'If a wife is ashamed of her husband's trade—'

They waited for him to go on. He glared from one to the other and stamped into the wash-house.

'You haven't taken your boots off,' Molly called after him.

'The broth's very good,' Harry said quietly, giving her a little look to let her know she was asking for trouble.

'I'm not ashamed of his trade at all,' she said, calmly determined as she cut the loaf. 'But I won't starve.'

'A bit of starving now and then is good for a man,' Will said, thumping his boots under the table to make sure she knew that he still had them on. 'Our work here is done for the love of it. Not for the profit.'

'I've learned that much already,' Molly said. 'And you haven't been loving it much down at Collins's farm this morning, by the look of you.'

'Look at your parents, with their thriving drapery business as you call it,' he said, with savage contempt. 'They look like a pair of overfed seals.'

Molly stood up and smacked his face hard. Then she burst into tears and ran off upstairs. Will glared at Harry.

'Not a word out of you, understand?'

'I haven't opened my mouth, except to put broth in,' Harry said, quietly.

'Bloody women!' Will muttered. 'We were better off without one.'

'That's what comes of holidays in Brighton,' Harry said, with a tentative smile.

'I told you to shut your mouth,' Will snapped. He leaned over the tin as if he was smelling it, counted the few poor coppers and slammed the lid down on them. He could hear her sobbing upstairs and glanced uneasily at the ceiling.

'Anyway, she's here now,' Harry said. 'And she cooks better than Aunt Nellie.'

Will stared down at the broth for a time, slid his chair back, took off his boots, threw them across the kitchen, and padded off upstairs.

Two hours later Will came jauntily into the smithy to inform everyone that spring had arrived. Molly followed him with the tea tray and apologized to Tom for having called him away from his work that morning to help carry in the wood. And Ted Pearce was to forget all about her suggestion for making walking-sticks to sell in Caxton market. Ted looked relieved and showed Will the spokes he had removed from the old cartwheel in the yard. Molly had been right. The spokes were almost ready-made for the rungs of a ladder.

'They're oak, too,' Ted wheezed. 'And Charlie Rampling is in need of a ladder. He was saying he'd be coming to see me about one.'

Will beamed at Molly and gave her a little pat on the back.

'That's the kind of suggestions we can do with.' And he gave Molly a knowing wink. 'Charlie Rampling pays very promptly. So there! Our little tin will soon be as full as it is empty.'

Will was in a buoyant mood for the rest of the afternoon. After tea, he put on his best suit to take Molly for a walk.

'We'll go towards Hopford. Then I can show you The Firs, where Conway Starke lives.'

'Oh! If we're calling there I'd better wear something a bit more—'

'We're not calling there. Just walking past, that's all. You don't call at a place like The Firs.'

'But you said Conway Starke was your friend?'

'Yes, he is – in a way. But I can't call there without being invited.'

'You've never told me – what does Conway Starke do?'

'His father is Colonel Starke – and a very wealthy man.'

'He won't be for long,' Harry grinned. 'Not the way Conway is spending his money for him.'

'That's enough!' Will said, sharply reproving. 'They're gentry, remember.'

'Is Harry coming on this walk with us?' Molly said, her eyes fixed on Will.

Will cleared his throat and pretended to wind his watch. He had only finished winding it a moment ago. Harry smiled inwardly. He knew why Molly was so anxious for him to go on the walk with them.

'I'll sit here and have a read, if you don't mind.'

Molly's face fell.

'It must be a good book,' she said, looking over Harry's shoulder at the title, *The Vagrant Heart*.

'It passes the time. Aunt Nell left it in the drawer.'

When they got back, Molly made a pot of tea and Will explained the principle of the internal combustion engine.

'Does Conway Starke pay you for all these repairs?' Molly enquired.

'Oh no, there's no question of paying. I like tinkering with them. Two motor cars he's got now, you see.'

'If he's such a genius, I don't see why he can't tinker with them himself.'

Harry fetched the milk from the larder to try and keep himself from laughing.

'You awful boy!' Molly smiled. 'What are you grinning at now?'

'It was the first motor car I'd ever seen,' Harry said. 'Conway Starke had seen to the engine himself. He offered me threepence to walk in front of it with the red flag.'

'Harry told him it would cost him that much in shoe leather,' Will said, indignantly. 'It's no laughing matter, girl. That's no way to talk to gentry.'

'Will took the threepence himself,' Harry explained, laughing. 'He walked seven miles in the hope of something going wrong so he could have a look under the bonnet.' He was laughing so much he spilled the milk. 'You tell her!'

'I don't see it is anything to laugh at,' Will said, icily, brushing a fleck of mud from his best trousers.

Molly wanted to know what had happened. 'The engine fell out.'

'So he didn't see under the bonnet, after all,' Harry chuckled. 'It was right on Lovell's Bridge. Carts and traps were trying to get past for hours.'

'Geniuses don't work with their hands,' Will said, as they sat before the fire drinking their second cup. 'It's what's going on in their heads that counts. Mark my words! One day in the future – Conway Starke will flabbergast the world.'

'He's flabbergasted his father a few times,' Harry grinned.

They sat on for a while, yawning and murmuring about this and that, and watching the fire die down.

'Perhaps life in the country is not so bad, after all,' Molly said, winding the mantelshelf clock. 'But ooh, it does make you sleepy at nights.'

She said goodnight to Harry with a careful little smile and gave Will an encouraging pat on the shoulder. As if he was an entrant in the final round of a sheepdog trial, Harry thought.

The two young men sat there in silence. Will filled his pipe, making a great palaver of folding a spill to light it, then evidently changed his mind and put the pipe back in his pocket. He stood up and ran a finger around his collar.

'Feeling the chain already, eh?' Harry smiled. 'She hasn't taken long to show us who's ruling the roost here, has she?'

'Nonsense! She's been as good as gold today.'

There was always tomorrow, Harry thought, and told Will he would save him the awkwardness of asking.

'You can have my room. As far as I'm concerned, four walls are four walls. I'll be just as happy in the back room.'

Will thanked him and hastened upstairs to tell Molly that it was all settled.

Harry was quite pleased with life as he undressed for bed. Women were no trouble at all, even if you hadn't had much experience of them. They were fickle, yes, you had to accept that. It was no use getting yourself in a stew over it. But it was different for poor old Will, he supposed. He was in love with her, or whatever it was he felt for the girl. Despite all his anger and stamping about, Will was completely under her thumb.

And Harry felt a new sense of power rising within him as he slid his hard young body between the newly ironed sheets. Molly's washing was a lot whiter than Aunt Nellie's, he had to admit. And she looked a lot better, too, that went without saying. And a nice little pair of apples; Aunt Nellie looked like a creosoted plank in that old brown frock of hers. And he pondered on something Tom had said to the 'young 'un' that afternoon.

'Splitting image? You've never heard of it before? It means a strong likeness to another body, that's what. Comes from the comparing of the two separate halves of a split tree. Take young Harry here. You could say he's the splitting image of his father.'

And Harry agreed with that. Yes, he knew he had the steel of his father in him. His brother Will had his father's name but he was nothing like him. Will was a bit of a Will o' the wisp, you might say. Like their mother perhaps. But Harry could only guess at that because his mother had died when he was born. And perhaps that had its advantages: he had never been under a woman's sway. No! And he never would be.

chapter two

Molly scrambled up the mound of long yellowing grass behind the terraced cottages that overlooked Lovell's Bridge and gazed in wonder at the dense unruly mass of bramble, holly and wild rose, the few poor twisted trees striving vainly to be seen beneath the smother of ivy and twining honeysuckle. 'The wilderness' Will had called it as they had oiled the guns. A harbourage for game, where pheasants, partridges and rabbits flourished unchecked. Seeing it now for the first time, thick with bluebells and violets, Molly thought it a glorious wild Heaven.

'If only we could clear a spot in the middle,' she called as the men topped the hill from the bridge. 'Just big enough for the three of us. A tiny house!'

'We're hardly fairies,' Harry panted, 'and this is no fairyland either. A house, indeed! With guns banging away and pheasants dropping down the chimney?'

'A harbourage for what you call pests,' Molly pouted. 'Just like you men. Encouraging the poor things to breed so you may have the sport of killing them.'

Harry had warned Will it would be a waste of time to bring the guns and bags. And he was right. At the very first flutter, Molly screamed and clutched Will's arm just as he pressed the trigger.

'Leave me, girl!' he cried angrily. 'There's cottages below. God, we're shooting game, not people.'

'We shot no one,' Molly breathed, thankful as she watched the partridge winging high above the bridge.

'Goodbye, little bird!'

'Goodbye we should have said up there at the house,' Will muttered. 'You should never have come if you can't stand the sight of them being killed. You'd have had one in the pot quick enough when we brought them home.'

'God will be happier with him flying up there than rumbling

round in our stomachs. Mmm, can you smell it then? A tang you'd pay good money to smell in the town. There it is, look!' And she pointed to the beech coppice where smoke was curling up. 'Oh, I'm so glad I came to live in the country. When I think of all the years I've wasted over a draper's shop. Come on, let's go and see what they're doing.'

And she lifted her skirts prettily and ran towards the coppice. Harry shook his head.

'Whatever they're doing – five minutes and she'll show them a cheaper way!'

'She'll settle down,' Will said philosophically. 'She's changed already in the little time we've been married.'

'Aye, and so have you,' Harry grinned. 'Poor little birdies, eh? Ah, well! Swede and turnip again for Sunday dinner.'

'Perhaps she's right,' Will murmured as they ambled down to the coppice. And he looked up at the passing clouds and smiled at a secret thought. 'I wouldn't like guns banging away at me if I was flying. And according to Conway Starke – men will be flying about up there before many years have passed.'

From the coppice came the sounds of the bodgers; the thudding of the axes, the warning shouts, the hacking of the trimming knives and the swish of boots through crisp leaves as they carried the saplings to the waiting cart. Then the cry from Molly.

Harry ran like the wind. A man held her wrist. Harry swung him round, booted the axe from his hand and caught him full on the mouth. The man fell back on the iron hook, tipping the tea kettle into the fire; lying there in the hissing steam and burning dust he raged about 'the interfering bitch'.

'Your tongue needs a wash,' Harry said, taking him by the hair. The man screamed as Harry held the kettle over his face. 'You're more a bitch yourself by the sound of you. She is a lady, you understand?'

Molly cried out in fear as two other men came running from the cart. But Will was there now and the men stopped short, one of them holding out a restraining arm.

'Will Farmer, the blacksmith,' he murmured warningly. 'He'd snap our necks like rotting twigs.'

'Harry!' Will said sternly. 'Leave them to their work.'

Harry threw the kettle into the fire. As he walked away he heard the man mutter that 'the lady' must be mad, wanting them to give up their living in order to 'save young trees'.

At Sunday dinner, Molly asked Harry if the broth was to his liking and cut him the largest slice of apple tart.

'Thank you for offering your room to us, Harry,' she said, smiling fondly at him. 'Will says you've had that room since you were born.'

'Not quite,' Harry said quietly, wondering what was coming. 'I lived with Aunt Nell till I was three.'

'Well, you've had it long enough to grow accustomed to it,' she said. 'So! Will and I will stay where we are in the back of the house.'

Will gaped and Harry was not his usual self that afternoon. He forgot his Sunday nap for a start.

'You've chopped enough wood there for a month of Sundays,' Will exclaimed, yawning his way into the yard. 'Couldn't you sleep?'

'She didn't have any sticks to light up in the morning.'

'What the hell's all this?'

'A clothesline, what else?'

'But there's one at the bottom of the garden.'

'He's thinking of all the mud I have to walk through,' Molly said at the teatime inquest. 'Try some of my jam, Harry.'

'But the horses come through that yard for shoeing,' Will said sullenly, taking the jam just as Harry reached for it.

Molly spoke with deliberate calm, like a nurse dealing with a sick and difficult child.

'Harry's thought of that, haven't you, Harry?'

'I've made a pulley so she can haul it up,' Harry said casually, as if the job had taken only five minutes. And he was careful to refer to Molly as 'she' to let Will know that he would have done as much for anybody on his one day off from work.

'It'll need to be high up if it's to clear Richards's big shires,' Will said, keeping Harry waiting for the jam.

'It's ten-foot six to the pulley.'

'God!' Will cried. 'The whole village will see everything I'm wearing.'

'At least they're white now,' Harry said. 'Lord knows what Aunt Nell used to do with them. Held them under the pump, I think.'

The following morning, Harry embarked on a new routine. He rose half an hour before his normal time, blackleaded the grate, fetched the water from the pump and set the table for breakfast. In the evenings, as soon as work in the smithy was finished, he cleaned his room to save 'her' the trouble, carried things that might be too heavy for her, set the table for tea, and if it was dark enough for no one to see him, brought the washing in. Then he scrubbed himself from head to toe in the wash-house, giving his nails particular attention – Molly sucked in her breath whenever she saw their nails at table – and brushed his hair until it shone like hers. Then, after tea, he would sit by the range hoping that Will would go out.

Two or three evenings a week Will went up to The Firs to tinker with Conway Starke's motor car engines, and on Saturdays he always went to The Plough with Tom and Charlie Rampling. On these occasions, Harry would wait for the front door to close, then go up to his room to change into his Sunday trousers and a shirt that had been crisply ironed by her dainty, capable hands. Then, as clean as Sunday morning, and with something of the soulfulness of that particular day about him, he would sit by the range, his best boots squeaking whenever he moved to remind her how handsome he looked. Sometimes he had to wait for her. She would be upstairs or in the wash-house. He would sit there listening and as soon as he heard her coming, would jump up and make a little performance of placing the chair just where she liked it, then watch the sewing-box from the corner of his eye to see if the first sock she drew out was one of his. He hardly spoke, unless to answer her, but sat there gazing into the fire, letting her know by his silence that he quite understood what she was feeling.

Married in haste! Letty Herring had done the same thing and thrown herself off Lovell's Bridge, hoping to punish her husband by making him push her about in a wheelchair for the rest of their lives together. But she had only broken her ankle and he had gone back to Australia. It had made no sense to Harry at the time. Now he understood it all too well. He felt like the hero in Aunt Nell's book, *The Vagrant Heart*, with its 'undeclared love' and 'sweet stifling pain' on practically every page. But there it was. She had married the wrong brother and there was nothing either of them could do about it. The die had been cast. The shoes had been wrongly forged and fitted, and like poor dumb shires who could not tell of the pain, they would both have to suffer in silence.

'I don't think your Aunt Nell had ever heard of needles,' Molly said, holding up a sock with a hole that a Christmas orange could have rolled through. 'With socks like these and those awful great boots you both wear, it's no wonder you walk about like old men.'

The next Sunday morning Harry coughed outside his room and came nonchalantly down the stairs in his Sunday black, his feet tapping lightly in a pair of soft brown boots. 'Where the hell did you get those?' Will enquired as they walked out to the trap they always borrowed from Charlie Rampling to go to church.

'I thought it was time I used up some of my savings.'

'Savings?' Molly said, alertly, and a gleam in her eye as she looked at Will. 'I thought all the money in this family was kept in that tin.'

They had an understanding, Harry explained; when Will went out of an evening and took spending money from the tin, Harry was entitled to take a copper or two for himself. Harry never went out. Consequently, he now had seventeen shillings and fourpence in a handkerchief in his room after paying Arthur Borrowford three and sixpence for the boots. They had been sent all the way from Germany by a relative and had then turned out to be a size too small. They fitted Harry perfectly.

'They may be all very well in Germany,' Will grumbled as he climbed up to the seat and took the whip. 'But we'll have some looks in church.'

Harry held up his arm for Molly to hoist herself up. He had

seen Colonel Starke holding up his arm in this manner for his wife when they left the church in the carriage and pair; Harry had been practising it in his bedroom.

'Thank you, Harry,' Molly said, with a particularly charming smile. 'You're becoming quite a gentleman.' In the smithy, too, they noticed the change in Harry. 'Here, watch what you're doing with that damn tongs,' Tom roared. 'You nearly had my hand then.'

Harry apologized politely. It was entirely his own fault, he said. At any other time he might have told Tom to keep his awkward old bony fingers out of the way. And when Ted Pearce complained that the missus was late with the tea, Harry reminded him that *Mrs Farmer* had other things to do besides waiting on them. For one thing, cleaning up a house that Aunt Nell had been visiting twice a week for donkey's years just to laze about in.

'I can do without her tea, thank you very much,' Tom muttered bitterly. In spite of Will telling her not to interfere, whenever she brought the men their tea Molly's eyes were everywhere; she asked about prices, how much was charged for a particular job, how long it had taken them to do it, how the cost was assessed and what the profit would be. Then she would make suggestions for saving time or putting to good use materials normally thrown on the scrap heap. As far as Tom was concerned all this went in one ear and out the other. His skill had taken a lifetime to perfect and was worthy of only the very best materials; he would not have proper work ruined for the sake of a few pennies. So whenever 'Miss bright-spark' came up with one of her 'tight-fisted notions' Tom would find fault with every piece of iron he laid hands on and the apprentice would go backwards and forwards to the scrap pile in the yard, fearing for his life, poor lad, in case Molly appeared and caught him in the act. She had already clipped his ear for helping himself to spoonfuls of sugar from the bowl she brought in with the tea. Now she carried the bowl around with her, the boy watching her like a hawk in case she clipped him another one just for looking at it.

After her teatime economy drives, Ted Pearce, who had

been well-disposed towards her when she had first arrived, would chisel away as if he had her head in the vice, hissing about the strangeness of women with a mathematical turn of mind and going on about the girls' school in Lewes, which in his opinion should have been burnt down years ago. There was no wastage at all in the carpenter's shop, Ted had assured her of that. All off-cuts too small to be of any other use were burned in the fire beneath the upright oven, when even heating was required for objects too cumbersome to be heated in the hearth of the forge. Molly had been satisfied, but Ted was convinced that she was 'wrangling her brains' day and night to think of some better use for the off-cuts.

'She'll be wanting me to glue the sawdust together next,' he said gloomily, sitting on the log alongside Tom to drink his tea. The log had been in the yard for years, the top worn smooth through use, and it made a pleasant seat for their break in the warmer weather. 'Or saw this log into planks. Who does the missus think I am – Samson?'

'The missus?' Tom tut-tutted. 'Mrs Farmer we must call her now, according to Harry.'

'Too many bosses here, that's the trouble. Will with the whip hand. Her, a little whip beside him. And Harry, only eighteen, and already thinking he's got the bit between his teeth.'

Ted should have had a carpenter's shop of his own, of course, he knew that. But it was too late now to think of buying tools and paying rent on a place where he had a wife and three children to keep. On top of the damn cough that kept him in bed for days on end.

They watched Harry cross the yard to the back door of the house.

'Taking his tea to have it with her.' Ted coughed, patted his chest, and gave a thin little smile. 'Not all he's having with her, according to some.'

On his way up to The Firs that evening, Will remembered his pipe and went back to the house. Harry, in his best trousers, his best shirt still unbuttoned, was pulling on his brown boots.

Will eyed him curiously. He had never known Harry to go out of an evening. Where was he off to?

'Nowhere! I felt like a change, that's all.'

'I see! Well – I shan't be more than an hour.'

'I've heard that before,' Molly said after Will had gone and she sat in the chair Harry had placed for her by the fire. 'Eleven o'clock gone and I'll be tapping my foot in that window. And Conway Starke not paying him a penny for all he does on those motor cars. Repairing them? He must be making them, the hours he spends up there. And that tin empty in the drawer again. Your brother's a fool. And look at me! Hardly married and I'm already a widow to the internal combustion engine.' She gritted her teeth to snap the thread. 'Well! I won't stand much more of this, I tell you. Just because I've got a ring on my finger . . .'

Harry felt a trembling in the back of his neck. She was not nearly as soft as he had come to think. It was no use blinding himself to the fact that she was a very determined young woman. And with 'town ideas'! Not the sort to suffer in silence for ever. A month or two at the most perhaps. And he had a vision of himself with Molly beside him, riding off in Charlie Rampling's trap, borrowed not for a Sunday morning only, but for a lifetime together.

'Come and live in the country, away from the smells of the town. He said nothing about the smells around here.' She threw Harry's sock into his lap and took her coat from the hook. 'Well! I'm not sitting here, night after night, staring at walls.'

Harry felt as if she had stabbed him.

'There are dogs about,' he said, thinking someone else must be saying it.

'Good!' There was a hard gleam in her eyes. 'I'm just about ready for a bit of bite and scrap.'

After she had gone, Harry sat there for a long time staring at the empty chair. Then he bent down and unlaced his boots.

Will had stopped at The Plough on the way back from The Firs and was in a jolly mood.

'You haven't been working, have you?'

'Not likely,' Harry said. 'But there's not much point in sitting around in your best clothes, is there?'

Will sniffed. What was the strange smell in the house? Harry couldn't smell anything.

'Well I damned well can. Here, what have you been burning?'

'Oh. Yes. It must be my boots you can smell.'

Will stared at him.

'You've burned your boots? Your new brown ones?'

'You were right! They look ridiculous.'

'What d'you want to burn them for? You could have sold them. What are you looking for?'

'The tea caddy!'

'You've just put it on the table.'

'Oh, so I have!'

Will's eyes narrowed. What was going on? Why had Molly gone up so early? She hadn't gone up, she'd gone out.

'Out? Out where?'

'Just out, she said. I don't know where.'

'You were here with her.'

Harry was silent.

'What's going on here?' Will roared suddenly. 'Can't I go out for two minutes without—'

'Without what?' Harry thumped down the caddy. The lid flew up and tea jumped out on to the table.

'Don't use that tone with me.' Will was breathing heavily now. His look was dangerous. 'All this scrubbing yourself every night. Best clothes and nowhere to go. Playing the gentleman! What's been going on here?'

'It's you!' Harry shouted, knocking over the caddy to make a proper job of it. 'You'll be getting her tongue when she comes in.'

Her eyes were bright. Her face glowing with the wind. She threw her coat on to the hook and then her arms around Will's neck.

'I've been walking and walking,' she cried, happily. 'Oh, the country's so wonderful, even at night. Even more so at night. You can smell it. And feel it. And all the sounds of—' She stopped, staring at the scatterings of tea on the tablecloth, the flagstones and the mat in front of the range. 'What the devil's going on here? Have you two been fighting? This is you, is it, Harry? You'll have to learn to control that nasty temper of yours. Look at it! Just look at it! Here I am wearing myself out to make a decent home for us and he does nothing but hinder. God! What on earth is that awful smell?'

Harry told her. 'Burned your boots? A brand new pair of boots on the fire? Here am I scraping and pinching for pennies and you toss three and sixpence on the fire just like that! Dear God, Will, can't you do something about this brother of yours?'

Up in his bedroom Harry tore off the shirt that had been ironed by her tight-fisted little hands, hurled it at the wall the giggling was coming from, and tossed and turned all night at the thought of the damn fool he had made of himself.

He awoke reasonably refreshed, made a proper job of his bed so there would be no comments, and then sat down on it to have a good look at the shame he felt for his thoughts and actions of the past weeks. He bore no grudge against the woman. It was all entirely his own fault. And he had learned from his experience. From now on he would be civil to her, yes, but totally indifferent. She would have no effect on him whatsoever.

He stood at the window, looked at the new day, and resolved that it would be a very different day indeed for Harry Farmer. He went downstairs to wash. And there she was. All open down the front. She screamed and flung the bar of soap at him.

'She is used to living in the town, that's why,' rasped Will, cutting the loaf as if it were Harry's neck. 'They don't bolt doors there because people are polite and knock before they enter. In future, you shall do the same.'

Harry didn't feel like breakfast.

'It's no use being thirsty,' Molly said, holding her front,

even though she was buttoned right up. 'The birds are pecking the tea in the yard. I swept up a quarter of a pound very near.'

Ted Pearce was at home in bed with his cough. Charlie Rampling was waiting for his barrow, so Will told Harry to finish that job off, leading him into the carpenter's shop like a dangerous animal who needed to be caged away from the others.

Harry worked with a will. He enjoyed a spot of carpentry for a change and tackling a job that taxed his modest skill enabled him to forget the shameful vision of wash-house-Molly with soapy water running down the apples that were bigger than he had imagined.

By eleven o'clock he had made and fitted the legs on the barrow and was whistling happily when she came in with the tea.

'I thought it was a blackbird in here,' she said, smiling sweetly over the biggest cup, which she always gave to Will. 'You're in need of a big cup in all this sawdust, I expect.'

He turned into oak and wondered what favour she was surely going to ask of him. But she just stood there, staring at the off-cuts. Harry measured for the handles and waited for her 'bright idea' to save 'wasting' the off-cuts to heat the upright oven. Still she said nothing.

It was so quiet in the smithy that he could hear the apprentice's careful broom in the yard; the lad had a mindful eye on Molly's washing after being scolded for raising clouds of dust. Harry was uneasy. He had no reason to feel guilty, but after the incidents of the previous evening and that morning in the wash-house, he didn't fancy Will coming in yet again to ask what the hell was going on between his wife and his brother.

After making the same simple measurement for the third time and seeing three different pencil marks all denoting two-feet eleven, he banged the length of two-by-two down on the bench, whistled loudly, and began to saw away at a piece of wood with no pencil mark at all.

When she turned to him there were tears in her eyes. He looked at her and carried on sawing. Everyone knew about the tears they put on, however womanless one had been brought up.

'I wish to hell I'd never come here to live,' she said in a tiny voice.

'Oh, yes,' Harry said offhandedly, inspecting the groove in the toe of his boot where the saw had cut into it. Damn the woman! She looked like a pathetic little sparrow done out of its crumbs. What kind of a fool did she think he was? And what was she after, anyway?

'Here I am, miles from all the people who love me,' she sniffed. 'They all stare at me in the village just because I try to make myself look respectable. They all hate me, I know they do. And now Tom and Ted Pearce hate me. Just because I'm trying to scrape a better living for us all. It's hardly fair! Do you think it is?'

Harry stared at her as she went on.

'I'm sorry about last night. Going off at you like that. And again this morning. But – well – you understand how it was this morning . . .'

Harry said nothing.

'I'm very fond of you, Harry. I am! Really! And I know you'll do something to help. I love him, you see. I love him so much.' Her eyes were like saucers. 'And now he's going up and up – and never coming down. I love him and I don't want to lose him.' She twisted her hands with the worry. 'Not now!' And there was a significance in that which Harry did not understand. 'Will says there's no danger in balloons. But there is! I know there is.'

'Danger?'

'They intend going higher than anyone else has gone before.'

'You mind your own business,' Will snapped, glaring at his brother across the tea-table. 'Upsetting her like this. She was as good as gold when I explained it all to her. And I told you not to mention it, didn't I, Moll?'

'That's what he's been doing up there at The Firs all these nights,' Molly said. 'And telling us he was mending motor cars. Tinkering with balloons!'

'We've been doing nothing of the kind,' Will said, rising

from the table and putting his arms around her. 'Planning it, yes! But we haven't bought the balloon yet.'

'How much is it going to cost?' she enquired, her eyes fixed hard on his. 'And don't tell me you can buy a thing like that for next to nothing.'

'I won't be paying a penny of it,' Will said. 'It's Conway who'll be buying it.'

'Thirty thousand feet?' Harry said. 'And you say there'll be no danger?'

Molly started sobbing.

'Some people might think it's not far enough,' Will muttered savagely. 'Here, where are you going?'

'I'm not staying here to be widowed,' Molly called as she bounced her curls up the stairs. 'Take your balloon to Heaven. *I'm* taking the first train back to Lewes.'

'This is your doing,' Will snarled at Harry. And he ran to the stairs. 'You leave this house and you don't come back.'

'Wild horses wouldn't drag me,' she screeched, already packing, and scampering around the bedroom like a caged parrot.

Will cursed as he slipped on the stairs. 'I've told you not to polish these damn stairs, haven't I?'

'You see!' Molly called in triumph. 'Thirty thousand feet? You can't go two yards without nearly breaking your neck!'

'Give me that suitcase.'

'Let me go!'

'Give me it, or I'll smack your behind for you.'

'You touch me and my father will be down here sharp,' she screamed. Then burst into tears. And as he heard Will crooning to her, Harry wished that he had not promised Molly his help. But he could not go back on his word.

The next day, Harry walked up to The Firs, crunched boldly along the gravel drive, made friends with the two mastiffs, and was shown into the drawing room by a house-parlourmaid who looked as if she had never heard of Becket's Hill, let alone lived in the village all her life.

'I shall see if Mr Starke is about,' she said, waving him to a large settee as if daring him to sit on it.

'Thank you!' Harry said, remembering that her father had died of drink. 'It's Mr Conway Starke I wished to speak to.' And he sank out of sight into the cushions. 'Not his father!'

'I'd better tell him what it's about,' she said to the chandelier. 'He always wants to know people's business. He may be rather busy, you see.'

Harry stated his business and while he waited, he looked around in wonder at the high-ceilinged room that must have been bigger than their yard – smithy and all, he was certain of it. The walls were covered with heavy, gold-framed paintings, Indian carpets, brass gongs, spears, elephant tusks and tribesmen's shields; and the mantelshelf, whatnots, and occasional tables were all heavily laden with Oriental ornaments.

'Balloons?' a voice boomed. 'What's all this about balloons?'

Harry peered around the side of the settee to see a tall, fierce figure in breeches, woollen stockings and a tweed cap, looming through the open french window.

'Good morning, sir!' Harry said, and jumped to his feet.

'Here, you're Farmer's other boy, aren't you?'

'Yes, sir,' Harry said, and was about to explain that it was the Colonel's son, Conway, he wished to speak to, when one of the mastiffs bounded in, sprang at him with man-eating joy, and bore him back into the comfortable oblivion of the settee.

'Get out, get out!' the Colonel barked, wielding his stick, and the whacked animal slunk out. 'My son's gone to Brighton with some friends,' he replied, when Harry had explained. 'Parasites! Spending his money for him. Or my money, rather.'

'In that case, I shall talk to him another time,' Harry said, standing up. 'I'm sorry to have put you to any trouble.'

'No trouble at all,' the Colonel said, and pulled a long, golden cord near the door. 'Fetch us some coffee, Rose. And some of those nice biscuits we had yesterday.'

Rose gave a little bob, and from the supercilious little smile she gave him, Harry had an uneasy feeling that she had known very well that Conway was not at home, but instead of telling him so, had invited him into the house on the Colonel's instruction.

'I like to keep up with my son's latest ventures,' the Colonel said. 'He's rather forgetful. And so I have to resort to asking his friends about what's going on in that brilliant mind of his. Oh yes, he's a genius, you know. He has ways of spending my money before I've even given it to him. Tell me about these balloons.'

He gazed out of the french window as if seeing the dreaded spectacle of a balloon alighting on the lawn, while Harry told him of Molly's fears.

'Well,' said the Colonel, 'I can assure you that your sister-in-law, poor woman, has nothing at all to fear. Ah, thank you, Rose. And tell Simmons we have a guest for luncheon. You will stay, won't you, young Farmer?'

'Well, I really ought to be getting back to the smithy . . .'

'Nonsense!' And he beamed at Harry as Rose smirked out of the room. 'Luncheon is the least I can do. After all, you have just saved me a very great deal of money.'

'You've ruined everything,' Will shouted. 'Conway will never get the money out of his father now. He wasn't going to mention the balloon until everything was settled.'

'Good!' cried Molly. 'It'll teach him a lesson. And keep you where you belong. Capering about in balloons, indeed. Your place is out there in the smithy. Earning a living for us.'

'What is it you think I'm doing now?'

'I don't know, I'm sure. That blessed tin is empty again, that's all I know. There's not enough work out there for keeping six people.'

'Five! I've told you before, we don't pay the apprentice a penny. He's learning his trade.'

'Learning to starve, poor boy. Five, then! There's not enough money for keeping five.'

'What do you want me to do?' growled Will. 'Sack Ted Pearce or Tom?'

'Why not?'

'Because I can't,' Will said, rising angrily from his chair and fingering his belt as if he would like to put it about her. 'There's no other work for them here in Becket's Hill.'

'Then let them look elsewhere. They can't expect us to pay them wages when there's no money left for ourselves.'

'We've always managed in the past.'

'Before I came, you mean? So I'm the one of the five who shouldn't be here, is that it?'

'Don't go packing your suitcases again,' Will said, wearily. 'Anyway, we haven't got your train-fare.'

'Very well!' she said, marching to the drawer. 'I'm going to earn my bread now. I'm going to do my bit of blacksmithing. This tin is melting in the fire, three generations' fingermarks or no.' And she danced her curls over to the range.

'Don't you dare!' Will roared, catching her arm.

'Let go of me!'

'Give me that tin.'

'You heard her,' Harry said, fiercely. 'Take your hands off her.'

'You keep out of this,' Will snarled. 'You've done enough harm for one day.'

'I didn't leave a comfortable home to come here and raise starving children,' Molly cried.

'Give me that tin.'

'You're hurting me—'

'Let go her arm,' Harry said, determinedly. 'If you don't, brother or not, I shall have to take steps.'

'Take a few now,' Will raged. 'Out of this house, you troublemaker.'

Molly tore herself free, and with a cry of triumph, flung the tin on to the fire.

'Give me that poker,' Will cried.

'Leave it where it is,' Molly panted, standing in front of the fire with her arms spread wide. 'The thing is happy there. It's as sick as I am of its poor empty life.'

'Get out of the way.'

'Don't you lay a hand on her,' Harry shouted. And, as Will pulled her roughly aside, 'I told you not to touch her—'

'Shut your mouth, will you?' Will rasped. 'I'm keeping her from burning herself. Her skirt is scorching here. Damn you, woman!'

His tone was severe but his eyes were like sheep's. She started to sob and he took her in his arms.

'Come on!' he said, gently. 'In the morning we'll have a good laugh over it.'

Molly smiled up at him and he wiped away her tears. Harry felt like an intruder; as if he no longer belonged in the house.

'As for you, brother,' Will said, harshly, 'you must learn not to interfere between man and wife.'

'You've ruined some more of my work, I see,' Ted Pearce said, giving the barrow a kick of disgust. 'I told Charlie Rampling he'd have to wait if he wanted a good job done. But there it is. Wheel it round to him and pick up the profit you've made out of my hands.'

It was little enough, Harry told him, by the time they had paid Ted's wages and the cost of the wood. Ted coughed and sneered.

'Trouble is, there are not enough workers and too many bosses. And no use you practising for one, either. Will is the elder. So you've no chance of being boss here. Unless you put a knife in him one dark night.' It was presumably a joke but from the way he leered at Harry it was as if they shared some dark secret. 'And then you'd have the little mistress to contend with, eh? But you could manage her well enough, no doubt.'

The man's mind was as nasty as his lungs, Harry thought, as he wheeled the barrow down to Charlie Rampling's. He had felt sorry for Ted Pearce once, but recently the man had too many black moods when he hated everyone and never stopped complaining about having to work for others when he should have had a shop and tools of his own. He had little to complain about, Harry thought, seeing they paid him for all the days he spent at home with his cough.

'I'm not handing over a penny until those handles are put right,' Charlie Rampling snapped. 'Here! Feel them yourself! They're hanging as loose as my old doings. If that Ted Pearce coughed one of his hard ones over it, the lot would fall to bits, I reckon. Take it back and tell him I want them handles done proper if I'm paying.'

'He didn't do the handles. I did them.'

'You? What the hell are you doing with carpentry work? Shoeing, your trade is! It's that woman up there. Profit-making again!'

Harry tightened his mouth and wheeled the barrow back down the path.

'That's not all I've heard about her, either,' Harry heard Charlie say to his wife as they went back into the house.

'You can do them yourself,' Ted said, a hard gleam of triumph in his eyes. 'You made them! Not me! You should have made joints. Know what joints are, do you?' He picked up two pieces of wood from the bench, and fitting the tenon into the mortise, jiggled it in and out. 'You should know how to do that well enough.'

Harry nodded slowly. He had been putting two and two together on his way back from Charlie Rampling's. He had recalled Molly's words about everyone in the village hating her and Ted referring to her as the 'little mistress'.

'Have you been talking to Charlie Rampling?' he asked.

'Oh no, not at all,' Ted said, smiling blandly. 'We discussed the making of this barrow by making signs with our hands.'

'You know what I'm talking about.'

'You obviously understand what I'm talking about,' Ted said, grinning evilly, and making the jiggling motion once again with the wood. 'They taught her a thing or two at that girls' school in Lewes that they don't know about round here, eh?'

'You watch your tongue. Or I'll nail it to one of your boards.'

Ted caught Harry by the throat, pushed him backwards over the bench, and held him there with powerful hands. Then he burst into a violent fit of coughing. When it had subsided, he sank forward on to the bench, lay there for a moment, then straightened up.

'A few years back, strong as you are, young Harry, I'd have held you down with one hand.'

'Who started this talk about Mrs Farmer and me?' Harry

asked, striving to contain the rage that was rising within him. 'Well?'

'Sam Rogett!'

'Who is he?'

'A bodger from Hopford way.'

Harry understood; the bodger he had punished in the coppice for taking hold of Molly's arm.

'I don't believe it, o' course,' Ted said quietly. He looked at Harry for a moment. Then he turned away, his body wracked with stifled sobbing. 'It's a hell of a thing. Knowing you're going to die when you've a wife and three children depending on you. And now this!'

'What are you talking about?'

Ted stared at him.

'Will hasn't told you then? He sacked me this morning.'

Harry picked up a chisel that had fallen to the floor during the struggle.

'Don't worry,' he said. 'You'll stay on here. If there's one too many in this place – it's me. And I've a mind to see a bit of the world.'

'The cavalry, eh?' Will said, as he sat at the table. 'No more shoeing horses for you, then. Sitting astride one with a lance. D'you hear that, Moll?'

'There's the dinner,' she said, ladling the broth into the bowls. 'But I don't know what we shall do for tea.'

Will and Harry smiled faintly at each other across the table.

'My news now,' Will said. And he looked like a cow with four calves. 'We're going to have a son. Alan, he's to be. That's right, isn't it, Moll? Alan William!' He held out the bread plate to Harry. 'The army! Fancy that! We shall miss him, won't we, Moll?'

She made no reply. Harry understood how she felt. With him gone it would be a better living for her husband and child. Women were selfish for their own. She had taught him that much. And he was grateful to her for giving him the impetus to seek a life that he now sensed was right for him, and which he would never have entertained if it had not been for her coming there. He would travel the world, not staying anywhere long enough to become attached to places or people. A man was better off like that, he thought. Living like the wind! Touching all – and abiding nowhere!

They ate their broth in silence. Then, at last, she spoke. There was a drop more left. It would be for Harry. To celebrate! There was gaiety in her voice – and a tinge of sadness, too, he thought. Or hoped for, perhaps.

'Yes, we shall miss him,' she said, and she tousled his hair. 'My! But he will look handsome in his uniform.'

*

Molly did not see him in his uniform, however, until four years later, when Harry paid them a brief visit on his return from South Africa.

'This is your Uncle Harry that you've heard so much about,' Molly said to yawning Alan William, who had been allowed to stay up late for this special occasion. 'He's got some toy soldiers in his pack – made them for you out of wood. Isn't he a clever uncle? And brave, too! He's been away in a foreign country, shooting a lot of nasty Boers.'

'I don't know about that,' Harry grinned. 'I shod a lot of horses, though.' And he winked at Will. 'We had balloons out there, Will. You and Conway Starke would have had a fine time.'

'You're not married yet, then?' Will remarked.

'A man is better off on his own,' his brother murmured. 'And it's no life for a woman – a soldier husband traipsing all over the Empire.'

When they saw him off at Becket's Hill station, he kissed Molly awkwardly on the cheek.

'Look after yourselves, both. And the young 'un there.'

'Your uncle's going now,' Molly said. But Alan William was more interested in the hissing steam and the whistling fireman damping down the coal. 'He'll be coming again soon, with more wooden soldiers, we hope.'

But eleven years were to pass before Harry's next visit. That was in the summer of 1912 . . .

chapter three

'You must get her up as soon as you can,' Conway warned, 'or you'll be in danger of hitting the trees.'

Will nodded from his perch in the birdcage of struts and bracing wires that festooned the mainplanes of The Flyer and gazed down the slope of uneven pasture land to the mounded turf of the boundary, topped by the thorn hedge. The elm trees were just beyond, their branches nodding in the light breeze as if to signal their presence and to underline Conway's warning.

It was a Saturday, a warm and sunny June afternoon, and almost everyone in Becket's Hill had come down to Collins's field to watch the blacksmith make his first flight 'alone and unaided'. Three weeks earlier, the sight of The Flyer in the air had created quite a stir and sceptical locals had taken a renewed interest in the strange machine. Back in the spring, she had trundled hopefully down the slope, sped forward with an ear-shattering roar, coughed a rude apology and buried her nose in the thorn hedge rather like an embarrassed pony who had suddenly realized it was not up to the jump after all. Further attempts to get The Flyer off the ground had been equally unsuccessful but not quite as spectacular, so enthusiastic interest had dwindled into vacant stares, the stamping of bored feet and wise old men yawning at birds who did it with no engine at all. Indeed, the sole and rather dubious pleasure of these outings had been to witness Conway Starke – one of the gentry, mind you – in tantrums you might have expected from a six-year-old faced with the Saturday morning senna tea for his bowels, and using language that some of the older villagers still refused to believe had come from the lips of a man who lived in the hallowed seven acres beyond the sternly imposing gates of The Firs.

But since The Flyer had first appeared out of the cloud over Lovell's Bridge, a new dawn had arisen over Becket's Hill. Conway Starke had become an airborne Christopher Columbus who had seen the roundness of the world by 'sailing' no further than half a mile – skyward! – and people were coming from all over Sussex to see the man and his machine.

Herding their way through a cattle-mucked opening in the hedge a party of Hopford farm labourers, whose curiosity had got the better of them, brooded on the queer-looking bird with bicycle's wheels and motor-car's mechanicals and decided she could never stay aloft despite Charlie Rampling having seen her 'whirlying' over Hopford square. They had obviously wasted an afternoon's rabbiting; and having recently watched a menacing demonstration of a threshing machine that could well put them all out of work, they hoped no one would see the possibilities of The Flyer's propeller for reaping wheat.

As on all such occasions, there was an expert; a chap 'down from London, over from New York', cap back to front in the best daring aviator fashion. He had ridden one of the Wright brothers' bicycles, spent weekends with Cody, knew Latham, Grahame-White and a birdman from Watford, and told the gaping party from Hopford that Will Farmer was in no danger whatsoever as long as he gave her plenty of hard rudder to avoid the two large bumps on take-off, pulled the control lever back soon enough to take him over the elm trees, was careful not to bank her too steeply in the turns, kept her nose well down coming in so as not to lose flying speed, and most importantly, of course, if any bits were to fall off, or if for any other reason the machine descended in a dangerous manner, Will was to make quite sure that he could distinguish the separate blades of grass before jumping out. The party from Hopford grinned for the first time; it might be better than rabbiting after all. The expert gave them a simple explanation of the theory of lift and drag with the help of a spot of algebra and moved off to enlighten the occupants of three motor cars arriving from Caxton; flying enthusiasts who had come to cut a dash. Brave braying and cawing young men who had never been up in a flying machine and who grinned maliciously at the storm-tossed sea of uneven turf, winked knowingly at the tallest elm, joked about snapping propellers and broken collar bones and going arsy-tarsy down the slope into the arms of some milky farmer's daughter. Then they swaggered their way to the oak tree where Arthur Rudkin, the grocer from Egerton Street, who had a flair for an occasion, was selling lemonade and boiled sweets at inflated prices.

Conway Starke had every confidence that Will would carry out to the letter what he had done on his three short flights under Conway's instruction. Will would take The Flyer off, rise above the elms with the Collins's farmhouse tucked away behind, turn her to port over Lovell's Bridge and fly straight and steady until he reached Hopford square, turning again to head for The Firs, Conway's home on the rising ground above Becket's Hill. Over The Firs Will would make his final turn, switch off the engine and float her down to rest once again on the safety of Collins's field. But with so many spectators present, Conway was taking no chances and he had paid six farm labourers a half-crown each to ensure that the crowd was kept back. If someone ran on to the field at the time of take-off or landing, Conway suspected that Will Farmer might well put the hardy bones of a Sussex countryman before the frail ribs of The Flyer. And that was a serious flaw in a pioneer.

Will had counted on spectators and was glad that he had put on his best, dark navy suit, pressed the night before by a tight-lipped Molly, and the black tie she had given him for his thirty-ninth birthday. Tom had muttered something about going to a funeral. The sarcastic old . . .

'Quite still! But not quite so serious,' Conway called.

Will smiled for Conway's new Kodak and thought it a pity about Molly. If only she had promised to watch from the yard; but she had made it plain she would not set foot outside the house. The greatest moment of his life and she would be baking bread for Sunday. Important things first, she had told him, and not to forget his cap or he'd bring home pneumonia. And what about Alan?

'It's all flying with him now. His bedroom nothing but glue

45

and rubber bands and a flock of creatures hanging from the ceiling. Any more and we'll have the roof down on us. He's leaving school soon and should be studying for his farrier's certificate. His shoulders over the anvil not his head in the clouds. Down there every evening in Collins's barn wearing his boots out on pedal-bars!'

'No need to worry over Alan. He's too young yet.'

'Yes, and you are too old. Like children with toys. And the work in the smithy going to pot. And supposing you came to harm – who would run the place then?'

Trust Molly to think of that. His brother Harry? No, Harry would never come back to Becket's Hill. Not after all these years. After he'd joined the Army, he'd seen service in South Africa, but now he was on the Reserve and working in a smithy in Wiltshire the last they had heard. A gypsy, Harry. Always on the move. Could never settle down. Should have found a good woman as he himself had done. But there, it was worrying over nothing. As he had tried to explain to Molly, of course there were crashes, crashes galore with flying machines, you expected it, but never more than a broken limb or two at the worst.

But Molly had refused to be consoled, and Will knew why. It was Old Tom and his damn magpies, going on about one for sorrow, two for joy . . . and he'd only seen one.

The old fool! Tom had been against The Flyer from the very beginning.

'There are millions of people in the world who have never even seen a flying machine,' Conway had told the old man when he handed him the drawings for the undercart. 'So you should think yourself privileged to be working on one.'

Old Tom had touched his cap and quite agreed. He could do nothing else. Conway Starke had money; at least, his father had. So Tom had fitted the bicycle wheels on the lengths of curtain rod and cursed Will Farmer's first visit to the flying club at Downside three years before. They were blacksmiths. Old Tom liked the feel of iron. He respected its hardness. Found comfort in its strength. It had to be hammered into shape, admitted, but once the shape was there, so it remained, and the article would last and give proper service. But this flying machine was just the devil's pretence of a job well done; bits of wood and wire married with waxed twine and hope, and the bad joins covered up with calico. A death trap and no mistake, for hadn't the creature already broken the legs of its previous master? That's why he had sold it to Conway Starke, who had got them all going like billyo for the past eighteen months making struts and bearers and God-knows-what and flattering Will into tinkering and spannering the whirling demon of an engine.

Old Tom looked at Will on the perch of The Flyer; the dark hair, swarthy features and heavy muscles encased in the dark navy suit, and he thought of a bluebottle trapped in a box-shaped web. For The Flyer's airy structure was little more than two box kites, one a third of the size of the other, joined by four 'longerons' or wooden booms. These booms, quite slender, supported the 45 hp Anzani engine with its gleaming propeller which Conway Starke was now preparing to swing.

A spindly man of thirty-eight, only son of Colonel Starke, Conway might have been considered elegantly sporty in his up-to-the-minute light tweed suit, fawn cardigan and patent leather shoes with cloth tops, had they not been thoroughly soaked in castor oil. According to Conway, castor oil was the ideal lubricant for rotary aero engines, and due to the principle of the rotary – the cylinders rotating about the crankshaft like a demon's roundabout – anything within champion spitting distance was assured of anointment. Conway had held his pilot's licence for just over a year and insisted that the health in his cheeks owed not so much to the lash of the upper winds as to the constant inhalation of this hot laxative spray.

'Switch on!' Conway bawled.

'Switch on,' Will repeated and clicked the switch. Conway swung the propeller and Will twirled the hand-starter magneto to boost the spark at the plugs. But all to no avail. The propeller snapped to a stubborn halt and Conway set himself for another hopeful heave, his weight on his right foot, his left trailing behind in a graceful curve, his fingers curled over the upper edge of the blade. He pulled sharply down and this time the Anzani shrugged undecidedly, responded to Conway's curse and rattled into life, setting the myriad wires humming, the cotton fabric trembling and tautening and startling the rooks from the elm trees at the far end of the field. Smoke snorted through the cylinders and whirred through the arc of the propeller lending a faint, steely hue to the gust that assailed the nervous jumping of the box-like tail.

Caught in the slipstream, women ran screaming, a dog barked after a rolling boater, and a newspaper floated into the air as if to herald the event that was to come.

Handkerchiefs waved, walking-sticks pointed and children ran up and down, whooping and clapping and urging their parents to take them closer to the noise. Will waved to the crowd, and hearing a special cheer just for him, gave himself up to the tingling excitement he had been studiedly ignoring ever since he had risen that morning, clock-watched to the dinner of Saturday broth and kissed away the frown on Molly's brow.

'Test your controls,' Conway shouted up. Will see-sawed the foot pedals to swing the twin rudders, moved the control lever back and fore, glanced at the waggling elevators to see that they were functioning properly and finally rocked the curious handlebar arrangement at the top of the lever. This caused the movable air surfaces on the mainplanes to rise and fall, working reciprocally, one going up as the other went down, to bank the machine in the execution of a turn. Everything was in order. He was ready to go. He looked back at Conway who was arched over the booms, his gangling arms spread out on the tail to prevent it rising in the oily ripples of the slipstream.

Conway glanced at the man and the boy at the port and starboard wingtips, their role to restrain forward movement until the signal to let go. The boy understood his function and grasped the wooden leading edge of the mainplane, respectful of the frailty of the tightly stretched covering. But Old Tom's fingers clawed at the fabric as if it had been woven by the devil himself. He cursed the creature, its owner and himself for being there. He had better things to be doing on a Saturday afternoon; needful things, proper work that you enjoyed and which earned your bread. Apart from that, that damn magpie kept fluttering about in his cagey old mind.

The cloud shadow moved swiftly along the primrose fabric of the mainplanes. The sun followed, streaming through the delicate structure and giving it the appearance of a strange butterfly.

With the power of an angry wasp, Will thought. It was time to set her free and his heart was pumping fiercely. He looked towards the dreaded elms and could see the newly whitewashed walls of the Collins's farmhouse through the leafy barrier. Someone scattered feed to the hens at the bottom of the yard. Collins's daughter Lorna, no doubt. She would be watching him soar over the trees. And Collins and his wife. All praying for his safety; for they got a generous rent from Conway for the housing of The Flyer in their barn. 'You'll never have the nerve for it, Will Farmer,' Collins had jibed. And Will had to admit he had thought twice that morning when one of the cylinders failed to fire. Soot on one of the spark-plugs. Would you credit it? – the greatest day of his life almost heeled into the earth by a paltry speck of soot.

'Good luck, Dad!'

And the boy waved. But Will heard and saw nothing; he was conscious only of his heart beating inside the Anzani engine. Eighteen months in putting her to rights, so his own life's blood was pumping the thrust into the whirring blades of the propeller. He *was* the engine; the great weight of her was engineered about his bones. Then, aware of the dazzling sunlight on his goggles, he was suddenly filled with an overwhelming emotion that brought tears welling up.

'Good luck, Dad!'

Will smiled broadly and waved a hand in return. A wisp of a lad for fifteen years, but the seeds of strength were there, bound to be from four generations of blacksmiths. He felt a pang of guilt as he caught his son's admiring smile. Molly had been right. He had let the smithy go to pot in order to play with toys. That's all it was, playing with toys, in spite of all Conway's fine talk of the pioneering spirit and the progress of man. The Farmer smithy was the boy's heritage and here was his father frittering it away. Molly was right enough, damn the woman, and she had fooled him into thinking she had not come down to the field because she feared for his safety. She was ashamed to stand there watching his antics amongst people who respected him. People who were waving and jumping about like lunatics at the sight of this foolish flying pierrot who should have been at the seaside doing a song and dance with bobbles down his front and fool's paint on his cheeks.

'Stand by!'

Will's pulse quickened. Thoughts of Molly, his son, his own foolishness, all vanished. His hands tightened on the control lever; his body strained forward so that like his machine he was an arrow on the string, waiting to be loosed. No Conway beside him this time. No shouts in his ear to correct some fall into error. No shove on the knee to indicate some urgent movement of the pedal-bar, or a pull on the lever to avert disaster. For the very first time he was to fly the machine alone.

'Let her go!'

The restraining hands obeyed and Conway dived on to the grass to allow the tail to pass over him. Like a loosed wild creature The Flyer plunged down the slope towards the elm trees.

Will rocked precariously as she bounded over the uneven turf, held his breath as the blades of grass became a blurring green torrent, then eased back the control lever. He thought he could hear the cheers as The Flyer rose into the air.

And she rose higher. Over the elm trees. Or almost! A sudden fluctuation in the air bounced her gently, and then, like a stranger in the dark coming across a step no one had bothered to warn her of, she sank with an uprushing sigh.

'God, I'm done for!' Will cried aloud as the axle of the undercart caught the leafy summit. In his anxiety to rise above disaster he drew himself up on the perch. The Flyer, miraculous it seemed, jolted upwards and Will thanked the Saviour for the puff of wind that surely must have come from

His own lips. The green moments of fright behind him, a guilty boy flashed through his mind, nesting for birds' eggs in a topmost branch when his father had already warned him twice.

'Blowing birds' eggs again, is it? You see this buisting iron? For marking sheep before grazing. I shall make one for you with a K – for Killer! For that's what you are if you go blowing young birds waiting to be born.'

As The Flyer soared upwards, Will's spirit soared with her. Oh, the joy of flying. The very wonder of it. If only Molly could feel as he felt at this moment, she would understand, surely? He felt as if his body encompassed the machine; he was not just soaring upwards, but in every direction, a million directions, dissolving in the air and floating like a cloud.

Seeing the church beneath the hill where God's hand had placed it so that its beckoning bell would echo both in Becket's Hill and Hopford, he thought of his mother buried there and wished he could pick out the headstone. Almost thirty-four years! He had been five years old. She had died giving birth to Harry and his father had told Will the sad news at home in the kitchen. The scene was so sharp in his mind. So well remembered. But he had imagined it of course, for he had recently found out that in fact he was staying with Aunt Nellie in Lampton at the time and his father had gone there to tell him of their loss. But imagined or not, the ache was always there, and a blessed ache it was, for out of it grew his deep love for Molly and his son.

Now he was over Lovell's Bridge. The turn to port. He pushed on the pedal-bar and eased the lever over, hearing the tinny bell sound of the ballpeen hammer again; this time for Molly as she walked down the aisle of the church beneath the hill on that other greatest day of his life. Oh, how he had loved her that day. Indeed, how he loved her still; how, how he loved her.

The Flyer straightened out, dropped and rode the air again, set on her course for Hopford square. A new and much colder wind blew through Will's dark navy serge. A wind from the sea, he felt, and blowing on a young Will's hopeful face. The holiday in Brighton when he had first seen Molly Grayson. She was standing on Brighton pier, clutching at her wide-brimmed straw hat and looking about her as if the ribbon that might have held it had blown away. He had watched and waited, hoping that the straw hat might blow away too so that he could run and rescue it for her. Then, when he had plucked up courage to approach her and offer his assistance, a woman in a black bonnet and veil had proclaimed that they were on a church outing from Lewes and hauled the girl away, leaving Will to spend the remaining days of his holiday mooning about the pier and studying maps and timetables for the shortest and cheapest route from Becket's Hill to Lewes.

As Will gazed out over the fabric of the mainplanes it struck him that their colour was so very like the straw of that wide-brimmed hat. Now wasn't that odd?

Something else was odd, for all he could hear was the eerie whistling of the wind in the struts and bracing wires.

'The engine's failed,' cried Conway, as if Tom and the boy were deaf. 'God, I only hope he keeps his head.'

The spectators were spilling on to the field to get a better view and Ted May ran up with a worried frown.

'We've asked them not to, Mr Starke.'

'Never mind!' snapped Conway. 'He won't be landing here. Not now!'

'An awful thing to happen. First time on his own.'

'It's not as bad as all that. He's into the wind. As long as he keeps her nose down and looks for a reasonable place to land, we may get away with no more than a busted undercart.'

'Him and his damned flying creature.' Old Tom's remark was intended to comfort more than complain. He smiled at the boy. 'Plenty of big enough fields that way, Alan, so he'll be fine, eh?'

The old man and the boy watched The Flyer gliding uncertainly on. The crowd was hushed and the boy could hear the faint humming of early summer insects as they droned over the grass. He wished one of them was his father and hoped he would find a reasonable place to land as Mr Starke had said. It would be a shame if he wrecked The Flyer. He looked forward so much to the evenings with her across the way in Collins's barn, sitting on the perch, working the controls as Mr Starke had shown him and pretending he was old enough to fly her.

'The bloody fool's turning in.'

Shocked heads turned as Conway ran through the milling crowd. 'Madam, for God's sake!' he cried, pushing a woman out of the way.

The Flyer was yawing around, her mainplanes waggling crazily.

'You'll lose speed and stall her,' Conway bawled, gesturing wildly up at The Flyer. 'Turn back into the wind, you bloody fool.'

'Language!' muttered Tom, looking uneasily around. 'Women present too.'

'He's right!' Alan said quietly. 'Dad should have kept her into the wind.'

'Your father knows what he's doing.'

They watched in silence as The Flyer hovered above the elm trees.

'He's got plenty of room to clear the trees,' Tom said.

As if in defiance of the old man's words, The Flyer dropped her tail, and like a falling sheet of paper alighted on the tallest of the elms. She steadied herself, jiggled as if trying to get comfortable and in total despair plunged nose down into the branches.

The crowd gasped, and the rending of fabric, the twang of parting wires and the agonized creak of the twisting booms were accompanied by the snapping and cracking of twigs as they fell aslant among the branches.

'She's come to grief,' Tom told the air – and he thought of the magpie.

'Months and bloody months it'll take,' Conway screeched as the crowd ran towards the trees, and a boy, in the hope of an encore, hurled a stone at a passing bird. 'I knew I shouldn't have let him take her up. I knew!'

'The selfish devil!' Tom growled. 'Money makes the mare

go. And damn well kills it too. Your father might have been—'
He stopped himself just in time. 'He's safe enough. The
creature's secure in that fork. The best place for her, too, I
reckon. See? Will's climbing out.'

Alan nodded gravely. Now that his father was safe his mind
had already turned to the rumpus when they got home. He
hoped his mother had burned the bread. Two disasters would
even matters up, and she might not have too much to say on
the subject of this one.

Will reached for the branch above his head in an attempt to
haul himself out of the shameful tangle of leaves and wreckage and cursed all the people who had turned up to watch for
not having better things to do with their Saturday afternoons.
And what the devil was Conway shouting up at him? This was
no time to go counting the cost, with whipping branches
adding further humiliation and bracing wires poking fun.

He tugged at the bending branch, glancing down at his legs
to see why he could not pull them free. The fork in which the
Anzani had come to rest was vaguely familiar. Ah yes! He
remembered now, a devil to get to, that one. A long 'shin-up'
from the trunk below. Had to unlace your boots and lace
them up again after, always a nuisance that. He had climbed
her three or four times as a lad. Bird nesting! And now he was
here again. Strange when you thought of it. He smiled at the
notion; this time he had brought his own bird with him.

As he tugged one leg free he heard his father's voice: 'Blowing birds' eggs again, is it?' A moment later he heard the
biggest bird's egg ever blown.

Women screamed at the explosion. A small boy leaped con-
vulsively, clapping his hands over his ears.

Old Tom wrenched Alan aside as the tree-borne wreckage
burst into flames.

chapter four

Harry alighted from the train at Becket's Hill station with an uneasy feeling that he might well be expected to assume the responsibility of the family business now that his brother, Will, was dead. Molly's son, Alan, was only fifteen. There was Tom Chater, of course; Harry hoped Tom was still working for them; he would be quite capable of running the smithy until Alan had finished his apprenticeship. Harry valued his freedom. A man was better off on his own.

'If you're going to Becket's Hill village, we've an omnibus now. She'll be along in ten minutes,' the ticket collector called after him.

The scene outside the station had hardly changed since Harry had left, fifteen years before. An omnibus was something new, at least. He wouldn't wait for it though. It was only three quarters of a mile. He needed to stretch his legs after the train journey and it would be good to see the old familiar sights. But he knew he was making excuses for delaying his arrival at the house. What could he say to her – a grieving sister-in-law who was now a stranger to him? He felt oddly like that awkward tongue-tied seventeen-year-old who had fled upstairs to change out of his dirty smithy clothes on the day she had first arrived at the house, and in spite of his apprehension and the mourning for his brother that was saddening his heart, he had to smile at the thought that she might greet him at the front door with firm instructions to take off his boots.

A short way down the narrow hedge-lined road a motor car honked behind a flock of bobbing black-faced sheep.

'Don't know what he's in such a hurry for,' the shepherd said as he lazed past. 'Train's gone, anyway. Just got off her, have you? Omnibus'll be along in a few minutes. Take you right into the main street.' And he stamped his crook and blared a curse at a hopeful runaway scampering towards the booking hall. 'Get back on the road, you black-faced devil.' Then he sucked his teeth at the honking horn. 'The omnibus is good as gold. But these horn-blowers want a stick about their backsides.'

Harry smiled to himself as he walked on. Everyone seemed anxious for him to take the omnibus. He understood well enough. A new service and a new topic of conversation. There was always one current topic that took preference over the weather, the harvest and the never-ending argument on the turning over of pasture land to the growing of wheat, so you knew exactly what people would say when you saw them approaching. That's what Harry liked about village life. In the towns they had too much conversation. They deafened each other with it. When he had been in the Army he could always tell the townsman at a glance; there was a drained look about him; as if he had talked the life out of himself in his anxiety to keep up with it.

As he breasted the rise just above Lovell's Bridge it was growing dark and the air was quite cold. He looked across the soft undulating pasture land towards the cluster of small houses and cottages that lay beyond the fields of Collins's farm and smiled at the shepherd's remark about the omnibus: 'Take you right into the main street'. Egerton Street! One could call it the main street, Harry supposed, even if there were only two other streets: Leadby Street, where Tom lived, and Haverton Lane. The Farmer smithy was situated at the very end of Haverton Lane, a little apart from the other houses, as if it had slipped away from them. There was no smoke coming from the chimney; it was too late in the evening. But of course, there had been no smoke coming from it all day, because in the little house across the yard his brother Will lay dead.

And he marvelled at the scene before him. How little it had changed! Nothing had been added or taken away since he had stood in this same spot eleven years ago when he had paid Molly and Will a visit on his return from the South African war. They had seemed happy and comfortable enough, with little Alan William, then four years old. How had Will died, he wondered?

He turned away from the stile and walked down the slope to Lovell's Bridge, stopping there to gaze down at the poor little brook. The downland soil drained easily, the rain soaking into the chalk and flowing away in no time at all, so small wonder the brook was so thin and shallow. Yet how deep it had seemed to him as a boy, coming out of the school across the way, taking off his boots and socks and hoisting his knickerbockers to wade in the 'deep waters'.

The sudden flutter of wings in the still air startled him out of his thoughts, and as he followed the pigeon's flight his eyes came to rest upon the church beneath the hill. Strangely, he had not thought to look at it until this moment; it was as if his eyes had been directed there to remind him of his omission. His mother was buried there in the churchyard. The woman he had never known. Harry's father lay alongside her. And tomorrow Will would be taken there to join them.

Harry saw no one in Leadby Street or Haverton Lane; the whole village appeared to be in mourning for his brother. Outside the smithy, a boy bowling an iron hoop stopped to stare at the stranger. Harry winked and gave him a ha'penny. Did Mrs Glover still sell home-made toffee? He had no need of an answer. The boy was already bowling like billyo to her house for the three-cornered bagful. Harry looked at the sign over the smithy doors: 'W. Farmer. Shoeing and General Smith'. It had been there since his grandfather's day; he had been William, too. He wished the doors had not been locked. He would like to have taken a look inside.

The curtains at the front of the house were drawn across the windows, upstairs and down. Tom, grave-faced, answered the door, looked at Harry for a moment as if wondering who it was, then shook his hand and took him through to the kitchen. Tom's wife, Alice, was preparing a meal for Molly's brother who had just arrived from Lewes, Molly's parents having arrived the day before. Molly herself was in the front room with Colonel Starke and Tom insisted on showing Harry in.

Colonel Starke remembered him, of course he did, and called him Albert as he shook his hand warmly. Molly, pale-faced and with dark shadows beneath the unseeing eyes, greeted him as a distant and half-forgotten relative and asked him if he had got the telegram all right. She had not been at all sure that he was still living in Tilsley. Harry started to explain that he was now living in Drayford and that the telegram had been sent on to him, but Molly went into the kitchen to tell Alice to set another place at the table. Harry was conscious of the photograph of Will on the oak dresser; he remembered it had been there the last time he had been in that room; eleven years ago.

'Your son took that,' he said, with a little smile at Colonel Starke. 'I remember how pleased my brother was with it.'

The Colonel smiled rather stiffly and suggested a stroll around the yard.

'She's taking it very badly. Very badly, indeed. I mentioned to her mother that she might take her home to Lewes for a few days. I told her – Alan can stay up at my place until his mother gets back. The change will do him good, too. Mrs Farmer's very worried about her son, you see. Understandably! The boy seeing the whole terrible business . . .' He saw Harry's uncomprehending expression. 'Albert, my dear chap, I'm sorry. But of course, you know nothing of it.'

And he told Harry of the crash and the explosion that had followed. Will had been so badly burned that he had died before he reached the hospital. Naturally, the Colonel was concerned that his own son, Conway, should have rebuilt the 'damned contraption' in the first place, and he paused as if fully expecting some recrimination from the victim's brother. But Harry was silent; too awed by the terrible vision of Will's body wreathed in flames. As a smith, working close to fire all his working life, he had suffered innumerable minor burns. He knew the agony caused by burning flesh and shuddered to think how his brother must have suffered during those dying moments.

The Colonel recalled that 'Albert' had left Becket's Hill fifteen years ago to join the Army and proceeded to talk at length about his own experiences in the South African war, bemoaning the introduction of mounted infantry.

'The Boers taught us the value of them, of course. But a damned shame. The cavalry has never held the same attraction for me since they began swapping lances for rifles. You're on the Reserve, I suppose?'

Harry said he was. And they wandered into the smithy, the Colonel battling and skirmishing his way through the whole campaign. Harry nodded politely, his eyes drawn to the forge, where a few blackened bricks had fallen from the arch since he had left there all those years ago. The hearth still contained the ashes of yesterday's fire. No! Saturday morning's fire it would have been, of course. The fire there in the hearth would not have been lit since the terrible fire that had burned his brother's flesh. What an agonizing death it must have been. No wonder Molly had looked as she did; her eyes unseeing, turned inward on the awful vision that Harry was imagining now.

After the funeral, Molly left for Lewes with her parents and Tom showed Harry around his garden.

'The goosegogs were the biggest I ever had. The change'll do her the world of good, as the Colonel says. She was fond of Will, you know. Fonder than she ever let on, I reckon. It'll take her a time to get over it. Alan's staying up at The Firs for a day or two. Colonel says he needs occupying. Taking out of himself. And he's right. A nasty sight for the lad to see, at the age he is now. Rhubarb's coming on. I shall look after things in the smithy until Alan's finished his apprenticeship. I've got Sam as striker. So we'll manage well enough. We've an omnibus now, you know – if you want to catch that earlier train.'

The old man could hardly wait to see him off, Harry reflected, as he stopped for the second time on Lovell's Bridge and gazed down into the waters of the brook. His presence had hardly been noticed. He should have felt relieved. But since the Colonel had told him of the terrible circumstances of his brother's death, Harry had felt a growing shame for the selfishness of his feelings. The more so since he had witnessed

Molly standing at the graveside. How brave she had been; how brave and how dignified. And how beautiful! He could never have imagined she would grow to be so beautiful with the passing of the years. She had been pretty, yes, with her doll-like face under the springing fair curls, the healthy bustling figure and the daintily capable hands. And he recalled those evenings when he had sat opposite her before the fire, thinking how much he was in love with her and believing she loved him; how heartbroken he had been when that dream was shattered. And he tried to compare the way he felt then with the feelings he had for her now. 'What feelings?' he murmured, and looked guiltily around in case someone had come within earshot. Watching her at the graveside he had been suddenly overwhelmed with a desire to comfort her; to put a reassuring arm about her, to tell her that everything would come right; that he would be staying to take care of it all. But there had been nothing to take care of; and she had hardly noticed that he was there. How strange that he should now feel so disappointed when he considered the dread he had felt upon his arrival at the house and how relieved he had been to hear the murmuring of so many voices when Tom had opened the front door. If only she had been alone . . .

'Uncle Harry!'

The voice startled him. Alan came panting up. Serious-faced, small for his age, with an engaging earnestness about him, and looking so very much like his father had looked years ago, Harry thought. He still had on the dark-grey suit he had worn for the funeral, and the cap, which he now doffed politely. When they had met that morning he had addressed Harry as 'sir' and Harry had felt more of a stranger than ever.

'Hello, Alan! What are you doing here?'

'I was going to give it to you up at the house, sir, but I thought it might be upsetting in front of my mother. Then I forgot all about it until after you'd left the house. My father would have wanted you to have it, I know.'

Harry looked at the pocket watch in the boy's hand.

'What about you?' Harry enquired. 'You'd like a pocket watch, eh?'

'It belonged to your father, sir. So I think it more fitting that you should have this particular one.'

Moved by the boy's sincerity and sense of rightness in deeming him the proper person to take possession of the watch, Harry thanked the boy, took the watch and looked at it in silence for a moment.

'My father wasn't wearing it at the time,' Alan said, as if sensing what might have been passing through his uncle's mind. 'Why, I don't know. He was never without it.'

'Neither shall I be,' Harry said quietly. 'Thank you, Alan.'

'It wasn't mine to give, sir.'

'For running all this way with it, I meant.' And he shook Alan by the hand, told him to take care of himself and of his mother, and apologized for hurrying off but he had a train to catch. He dared not look back until he reached the crest of the rise in case the boy should see the tears in his eyes.

Alan returned his uncle's farewell wave, watched the tall, stern-faced figure disappear down the other side of the rise and decided to walk the long way round to The Firs. He was curious to see his father's grave now that it had been filled in.

In the far corner of the churchyard a girl was just in the act of bending over the grave. She had her back to him but Alan could hardly have failed to recognize her. He had sat behind Lorna Collins for two years in Lovell's Road school; it would have been three but for Charlie Samuels refusing to swap desks. She turned with a start and Alan apologized in a low voice.

'I'm glad there were a lot of flowers,' she said. 'They do look nice, don't they?'

'Yes, they do,' Alan said, his eyes fixed on the newly placed posy of wild flowers. He was uncertain whether to thank her or not. 'My father was always fond of wild flowers.' It wasn't too much of a lie, he thought.

'I have to go now,' she said, at last.

'So do I. I'm to stay up at The Firs for three or four days.'

'Gosh! The Firs! Are you excited?'

Alan smiled calmly and said that he was. Neither of them spoke again until they reached the cart-track leading up to the Collins's farmhouse.

'Thank you for walking with me,' Lorna said. 'Goodbye!'

They both took an extraordinary interest in the sky and the earth as they walked their separate ways. Alan turned expectantly when she called his name.

'I'm sorry about your father,' she cried. And ran off.

At dinner, Mrs Starke made a great fuss of Alan and looked guiltily down at her plate as her husband explained that their son, Conway, was away on business and would not be returning during Alan's stay at the house. Alan considered carefully before he spoke.

'It was a shame about your son's flying machine,' he said. 'After all that work.'

Later, in the study, the Colonel outlined the exciting programme he had planned for Alan's stay; riding, shooting game, and, as Alan took such an enthusiastic interest in the cavalry sabres on the walls of the study, he promised to teach him the rudiments of sabre fighting. 'Perhaps when you're older, you'll follow your uncle's example, eh? Join the cavalry.'

'That won't be possible,' Alan said, as they browsed through the Colonel's large collection of books on military matters. 'When I've finished my apprenticeship, I shall have to run the smithy. The fifth generation. And I've my mother to think of.'

What a fine young lad he was, the Colonel thought, and as the evening wore on he was increasingly impressed by Alan's sharp intelligence, the way he carefully weighed matters before venturing an opinion, his directness of speech, the inner stability reflected in the unwavering gaze of the eyes. And he mused on Molly Farmer's deep concern for her son.

'To have seen it happen ... a terrible thing for a boy to have in his mind ... if he had been very young or much older ... but at the age he is now ... it's a difficult age, isn't it?'

And his curiosity having got the better of him, he ventured to ask Alan how he felt about his father's death.

'It's a shame for my mother,' Alan said. 'She will miss him. So will I.' He studied an artist's impression of two cavalry officers studying enemy troop movements and entitled 'The

Eyes of the Army' before he went on. 'Mr Starke was right. My father should never have turned back to land on Collins's field. He should have stayed into the wind and maintained flying speed.'

After marvelling at the comfort of his bedroom and the view from the window, where, in the moonlight, he thought he could just make out the roof of the smithy at the end of Haverton Lane, Alan knelt by the large bed and prayed for the soul of his father. As a small boy, he had been taught to pray in this manner by his father, and he had done so every night since his father's death.

He had an uneasy feeling that because his father had burned to death his soul might have been directed towards 'the other place'. And undeservedly so. His father might have been foolish – as Alan's mother had so often said – but he had been a good and kind man. Anyway, his soul belonged 'up there'. As he climbed into bed Alan added a short hopeful prayer for some miraculous combination of circumstances in the future that would enable a young man who had not been lucky enough to be born into the 'gentry' to enlist in the 'cavalry of the clouds'. It had been formed less than one month ago and had its headquarters on Salisbury Plain; the British Army had named it the Royal Flying Corps.

chapter five

Old Tom reckoned there was bound to be a war. You only had
to look at the Germans in the magazines to see that war must
come. He mistrusted their faces; that insolent air of challenge
about them. Those spiked helmets in themselves were enough
to provoke a war. And the goose-step marching, apart from
revealing the arrogance of their bullying nature, let you know
the direction the boot would be coming from. Belgium might
be caught on the backside, or France even, but 'dear old England' was well-prepared. Alan disagreed.

'Three quarters of a million men. But they're scattered all
over the world.'

'They'll be home soon enough when there's a war to be
fought,' Tom retorted. 'And the British Army is the finest in
the world. We taught the Boers a lesson they won't forget in a
hurry.'

'They taught us one or two, as well.'

'Such as?'

'That our cavalry's out of date.'

'Oh, aye,' Tom growled. 'The Royal Flying Corps again, is
it?'

'The aeroplane will be a big influence in the next war,' Alan
said with a knowledgeable air.

Old Tom sniffed. The boy was getting 'uppish' since he had
been going up to The Firs. And he reminded Molly of the fact
when she paid him his wage that afternoon. He was always
anxious to hammer home his grouses on Friday afternoons.
He had started work at the Farmer smithy as a boy of twelve,
pumping the bellows for Alan's great-grandfather, and with
sixty years' experience he was 'the kingpin' of the smithy. He
bought the materials, dictated how and when the work would
be done, assumed responsibility for the quality of the work-

manship, and was, in short, 'the boss'. But he was not the owner. He was still an employee and resented the fact even more since Will Farmer's death. A wage held out to him in the hand of an owner who contributed nothing towards the running of the smithy – and a woman's hand at that – was doubly galling to him.

'That boy of yours is becoming too good for the rest of us here,' Tom grumbled, drawing his apron aside in order to shove the hated wages into his trouser pocket. 'And you know where it comes from, don't you?'

Yes, Molly knew. And she was grateful to Colonel Starke for all he had done to help Alan in that difficult period soon after her husband's death.

'Just like his father and Conway Starke,' Tom said, disgusted with himself for worrying the woman with such a comparison. 'And you remember how that ended up. A man should be content with his station and not go trying to rise above himself.'

'There's not much wrong in Alan learning proper manners from a gentleman,' Molly said tartly, hoping to remind him that he had taken his wage without so much as a 'thank you'. 'And as the shoeing trade depends as much upon the local gentry as it does upon mumbling farmers, I should have thought his learning to speak properly might well be to our advantage.'

Feeling her words were a slight on his own 'mumbled' speech when in the presence of the likes of Colonel Starke, he told her that the war would put paid to the shoeing trade from the gentry. The Colonel himself had said that in the event of war coming, horses not gainfully employed in farming would be compulsorily purchased by the Army.

'War, war!' Molly said, uncommonly angry. She had been so long in the grey world of grief and was just discovering the joy of living once again. This talk of war pushed her back into those dark months just after Will had died, when, alone and despairing, she had lived their lives over and over, spiralling down to a depth from which she was certain she would never be able to rise. If it had not been for Alan she would never have survived, she was certain of that. She had never confessed as much to anyone, of course. No, that would never have done. She had put on a brave face; as was expected of anyone in such circumstances, she knew that. The grief, now almost faded, had become a wonder to her. How strange it was to have loved a man so much and to have realized it only when he was dead. And he had been no extraordinary man by any means. Why had she loved him so much? For his foolishness, perhaps? The foolish whims she had always chided him for and which had finally accounted for his terrible death? 'You men! Can you find nothing else to speak of but war?'

'It's no use shutting our eyes to it,' Tom said, damping down the fire with the sprinkling can and dwelling on the disturbing thought that he had lived through so many wars and had never heard a shot fired in anger. He was glad he had no son. The shame he would have felt in trying to explain it away. 'Alan can't wait for it to start.'

Molly felt a sudden chill at his words.

'What do you mean?' she asked.

'He reckons we'll see the outbreak of hostilities as he calls it before the harvest is in. But he's wrong there.' And the old man gave a little superior smile. 'I'm never far out in my predictions, as you know. There'll be a war right enough, yes. But it will take its time in coming to the boil. With luck, peace will hang on till the spring of next year. At any rate, there'll be no war this year, that's for certain.'

And most of the country agreed. War was inevitable. But not imminent. It loomed as a dim spectre for gloomy pacifists and as a threat too far away for the ever-hopeful militants who had hungered for it ever since the end of the South African war, a desultory affair that had done little more than whet their appetites. Those who held up their hands in horror at the possible holocaust of a European conflict were told by the advocates of bloodletting that the Empire was in dire need of war in order to recover from the bloating years of peace. Its honour had faded in the far-flung outposts, its glory worn to a shadow under the sun that never sets, and neither could be restored in further ignominious skirmishes with tribesmen or the quelling of minor rebellions that commanded only a half a dozen lines at the bottom of a column in *The Times*. No, what was needed now – indeed, it was absolutely imperative – was a great and glorious front-page European conflict.

It came much sooner than anyone expected and by the end of July the young manhood of Europe was reporting in its millions to regimental depots. Eight armies were forming in Germany and five in France. Britain, whose prime consideration was to uphold the neutrality of 'brave little Belgium', was the last to mobilize. On the first of August, in order to safeguard Channel crossings, the Admiralty ordered full mobilization of the fleet, and when it was learned that German troops had violated Belgian territory, the War Office made public the general mobilization order.

On the ninth of August, the British Expeditionary Force, under the command of Field Marshal Sir John French, had begun to embark for France to take up positions between Maubeuge and Le Cateau. Among them, viewed with curiosity and amused disdain, was a small group of officers of the Royal Flying Corps: their purpose was to look for suitable landing grounds for the four Squadrons which were preparing to leave for France. 'To help the enemy,' one General Staff officer put it. This view of the ill-trained men of the Royal Flying Corps and their ludicrously inadequate flying machines was held by many.

*

'If the General Staff hadn't been so stubbornly against the aeroplane from the very beginning, they wouldn't be looking down their noses at us now,' Captain Triggers exclaimed to his observer, Lieutenant Sears, as the morning parade was dismissed.

There had been an air of fevered anticipation ever since the parade had been announced. Morning parades in the RFC were something special, the still air of the early hours being too precious to be wasted in standing around. This was the safest time for flying; and very often the only time for those undergoing training in the Maurice Farman 'Longhorn', for once the wind got up she was far more difficult to control and the number of crashes was already alarmingly high.

'So we're to stand by to fly to France, eh?'

'Did he mean the whole Squadron was to fly over together?' Sears enquired casually, as if he had no qualms at all about finding his way there. Sears had only recently been seconded from his cavalry regiment, being told that reconnaissance from an aeroplane was no more difficult than reconnoitring on horseback with field glasses; but he had learned the falsity of this, having lost his way during six of his seven cross-country flights and been violently ill on all seven occasions. 'I mean, we're not going singly or anything, are we?'

'I don't know what you're so worried about,' Triggers grinned. 'The roads, villages and all the other things that you insist look alike from up there – there'll be none of those to confuse you, will there? Just plain water all the way.'

Sears smiled and looked relieved. Until he thought about it.

'Where are we supposed to cross the French coast?' he asked.

'That doesn't bear thinking about. As long as we reach it, that'll be good enough for me. I can't swim, you see.' And he clapped Sears heartily on the back. 'Just stop worrying, eh? We'll get to Amiens all right.'

'It's all very well for you,' Sears said glumly as they went into the Mess for breakfast. 'I'm just a fledgling. But you – you're the second oldest bird on the Squadron.'

And that was true enough. Triggers, then an officer in the Royal Engineers, had been bitten by the flying bug whilst on leave in France in the summer of 1911. He had looked on spellbound at two machines giving a display and had made up his mind there and then to be a pilot. One of those machines was a Farman, the type of machine Triggers now flew as Commander of 'C' Flight.

Which just goes to show how far ahead of us the French are, Triggers thought. He had cut short his stay in France and spent the remainder of his 1911 leave learning to fly with the 'Aero Club of the United Kingdom'. He had returned from leave the proud owner of the Aero Club's pilot's certificate and had immediately applied for attachment to the newly formed Air Battalion, and when the Royal Flying Corps was formed a year later, was given command of 'C' Flight.

'Two years,' Sears commented. 'I should have thought you might have been commanding the Squadron by now.'

'I'm not the right chap for a Squadron Commander,' Triggers said. 'I'm too famous for my crashes.' And seeing Sears's uncertain smile, assured him that most of these had occurred whilst he was flying alone. He didn't take chances when he had an observer flying with him. 'I like experimenting. All the things we're told an aeroplane can't possibly do.' And he sighed. 'They're right. You certainly can't put too much stress on any of the ill-assorted collection of death-traps they're sending us to France with.'

Sears grimaced and pushed his plate aside. 'I bet French Mess lunches are a damned sight better than ours,' said Triggers, as they got up and went through to the Mess lounge for their coffee.

Triggers looked thoughtful. 'Aside from my reputation as a crash merchant – I suppose they consider my temperament is not quite ideal for a Squadron Commander.'

Sears sipped his coffee and made no comment. He had known Triggers for little more than three weeks but had already been the victim of his violent temper on at least four occasions. Triggers was charming and immensely likeable but one felt the presence of a controlled ferocity which was liable to erupt at any time. In spite of this, Sears would not willingly have changed places with any other observer in the Flight. Insecure in his lack of knowledge and experience in the air, Sears felt himself to be in safer hands with Triggers than with any other pilot on the Squadron. And the man's ebullience and fierce bravery seemed to be rubbing off on him; Sears was gaining in confidence with each successive flight in the company of Triggers. Again, he knew that although Triggers had a contemptuous disregard for his own personal safety, in a time of hazard he would have the highest regard for the life of his passenger.

'The English have never been very good at preparing for war,' Sears said, in defence of the Government's years of procrastination with regard to the aeroplane as an integral part of the British Army. 'I mean, look at Drake – playing bowls before tackling the Armada.'

'Yes, but he didn't have to fly a piece of machinery that was an enemy to begin with, did he?'

'We're not a nation that longs for war. So when it comes – well, we have that feeling of right being on our side, if you know what I mean. A confidence in the virtue of our cause.'

'I'd sooner have confidence in a machine I could fly at more than sixty miles an hour knowing that the wings wouldn't fall off,' Triggers said, as they walked over to 'C' Flight office. 'If the General Staff had opened their eyes to the value of aeroplanes a few years ago, we could have developed at least one good machine to be flying to France in. And we wouldn't be quite the despised force we are at the moment.' He went on to explain to Sears that as early as 1911 the Italian army had realized the value of their small aviation detachment in the Turko-Italian war. Flying French aeroplanes, the Italian pilots carried out reconnaissance flights, directed gunfire from battleships and mountain artillery, and had even dropped small bombs to good effect. Surely that should have been enough to convince the General Staff and the British Government of the aeroplane's value as an instrument of war? But no, even now it was still regarded by many as a useless and expensive fad; a toy for wealthy sportsmen.

'It's not as if aerial reconnaissance was something new,' Triggers said, as he waited for the members of his Flight to assemble. 'Two Royal Engineers' officers badgered the War Office to use balloons for reconnaissance in the middle of the last century. But they got no encouragement whatsoever. However, balloons proved their value in the end. That spot of trouble in Bechuanaland.' And he grinned. 'The natives were very impressed with the balloon detachment. One of the chiefs went up in one. "The English have great power," he said. And he had a hell of a lot more foresight than our War Office!'

'It's a painful process, I suppose,' Sears said. 'Assimilating noisy, smelly machines into the Army tradition.'

'Going to be a lot more painful for us,' Triggers snapped. 'Flying over the German lines in those machines of ours. The Germans haven't been marking time. You can bet your life on that. They'll have a thoroughly efficient air force by now. Certainly equal to the French – if not better. They're not going to sit back and let us gather information at our leisure, are they? No, indeed! We're going to have to fight for it. Even the War Office could foresee that much, I imagine.'

The Flight was now assembled and Triggers addressed them. He explained that while they were awaiting their final orders to fly to France, they would carry out patrols along the coastline on the watch for possible attacks by enemy aircraft.

'Count Ferdinand von Zeppelin's cigars, we mean, of course. They're the only type of German aircraft capable of attacking us. At least, as far as we know.'

'God, they don't really expect us to shoot down Zeppelins with one of these, do they?' Sears enquired, looking despairingly at the Winchester repeating rifle.

'*And* two rifle grenades, sir,' the armoury sergeant put in, placing them on the counter. 'You might make a better hole with one o' those, sir.'

'Two? Is that all?'

'There's a shortage, sir.'

'They've caught us with our trousers down,' Triggers said, picking up a bandolier of fifty rounds, then a Scott-Webley revolver. 'This should give the Hun a laugh.'

The mention of 'trousers down' reminded Sears to pay a visit to the latrines before take-off.

'I always forget you can't go once you get up there.'

'And take your spurs off while you're about it,' Triggers called after him. 'Unless you're planning on dropping on to the Zeppelin and riding him home.'

In the latrines Sears met the Squadron Commander who told him, 'There's no problem at all about your rifle being ineffective against a Zeppelin. They fly considerably higher than your Farman so they're well out of your range, anyway.'

'So what's the point of patrolling?' Sears asked Triggers later, as the two of them climbed into the nacelle of the Farman. 'I resent being as sick as a dog when we might just as well have stayed on the ground all afternoon!'

'Zeppelins *can* fly higher than us, yes. But we don't know that they *will* be flying higher, do we? I mean we don't know what their orders are. But you're right about the rifle. Useless, obviously. The grenades might be better. But really, I suppose, there's only one certain way if we could get close enough.'

'What's that?' Sears asked, with a feeling of dread.

'Well! We could ram her! That might convince the General Staff that our aeroplanes are of some use!'

Sears laughed uncertainly.

'Never mind the damn machine,' he said. 'What about us?'

'At least we'd save a lot of innocent people being bombed,' Triggers said. Then he grinned at Sears, whose stomach was turning over before the propeller had even been swung. 'Don't look so worried. It was just a thought, that's all. I'm not the stuff heroes are made of. In any case, I want to live long enough to see aeroplanes prove their value in this war.'

They droned over Chatham dockyards for the next two days without seeing a sign of a Zeppelin. Then the impatiently awaited order came through; they were to fly to France. They would proceed to Dover where a landing-ground had been prepared, refuel and carry out any necessary repairs, then fly to Amiens. Each man was issued with field glasses, a Scott-Webley revolver, a roll of tools which might assist them in case of a forced landing, a spare pair of goggles, a water bottle, a small stove, and, in his haversack, biscuits, cold meat, a piece of chocolate and a packet of material for making soup.

'God!' said a red-faced pilot after dumping the lot down on his cot that night. 'We shall never get off the bloody ground, let alone fly to Amiens. What the hell do we want with a stove?'

'You can always chuck it at a Hun aeroplane if you meet one,' his observer grinned. 'We've little else to defend ourselves with.'

'We take off at dawn,' Triggers said, coming into the hut.

'You'll all follow your leader, of course, but you'll have enough sense not to follow me if I come down in the Channel or have to make a forced landing in a ploughed field.' This was greeted with laughter. But Triggers looked serious. 'It's happened before, as you all know. So let's use our common, eh? We don't want to make ourselves more of a laughing-stock than we already are in certain quarters.'

'What about all the equipment, sir?' enquired Lieutenant MacEwen, a ginger-moustached young pilot who wore the tartan trews of a Scottish regiment. And seeing the doleful glances at the little mountains of issued equipment on the beds, he added, 'I mean all the stuff necessary to keep us flying, sir? Hangars, spare engines, motor transport and so on?'

'That's not our problem,' snapped Triggers. 'There will be a suitable Aircraft Park set up for supplying airfields with their needs and to carry out major repairs on our machines. Where that will be – or indeed, where we will go on to from Amiens – I'm afraid I can't tell you. And I doubt if there is anyone at this moment who knows where our airfield will be. My feeling is that for a short time, at least, we shall be moving around a bit. You play the violin, don't you, Caswell?'

'Yes, I do, sir,' Caswell piped. He blinked and looked rather bewildered. 'But I wasn't taking it with me. I don't think there'll be room.'

'I should make room,' Triggers said. 'And I should practise a Cazardas or two. As we're going to be living like gypsies, it might help to put us in the right mood. And if it's any con-solation to you all, I imagine Field-Marshal Sir John French is just as uncertain of his ultimate destination as we are.'

The following morning Triggers's Flight set off for Dover. Second-Lieutenant Caswell crashed his BE2 on take-off and was killed instantly, along with his observer. The crews of the three remaining machines were issued with motor-car inner tubes before leaving Dover for Amiens two days later.

'At least they'll keep us afloat long enough to regret having ever left the Engineers,' Triggers said to his Squadron Com-mander, who was the 'oldest bird' in the Squadron, having transferred to the old Air Battalion two whole months before Triggers.

Hampered by a dud cylinder, Lieutenant MacEwen's machine was left behind on the cross-Channel flight and made a forced landing five miles east of Le Havre. The combination of the Lieutenant's tartan trews, schoolboy French spoken with a thick Scots accent, and the fact that his Blériot had been used for civilian advertising purposes and had the letters HOR on the underside of one wing and LICK'S on the other, resulted in MacEwen and his observer spending five days in a French jail. 'I shall never drink malted milk again as long as I live,' MacEwen complained when he eventually rejoined Triggers's Flight at the Squadron's temporary airfield near Maubeuge. 'And the machine I was flying was a Blériot – a French machine! How on earth they could have thought I was a German spy ...'

'No one knows one machine from another,' Triggers explained. 'We've found that out to our cost already.'

He showed MacEwen his Farman, which looked like a flying colander. Riggers were mending a bullet-smashed strut and severed bracing wires.

'When the French opened up, I assumed no one had bothered to tell them we were on their side. But then the British infantry greeted us with a roar of musketry this afternoon.' And he grinned. 'I didn't think the War Office hated us quite that much.' Indicating the tins of paint being carried from the Crossley tender, he added, 'The Squadron Commander's got everyone on painting duty this evening. Union Jacks on the undersides of the wings. We should have had them stitched on before we left England. No one thought of it. Incredible, isn't it?'

'Just the undersides?' MacEwen said reflectively. 'Someone told me the Hun flies higher than we do. So he won't see the Union Jacks, will he?'

'I'd have thought that was in our favour. If he's assured we're British – well, he might go taking potshots at us.'

'What about French pilots though? Won't it worry them – not knowing whose side we're on?'

Triggers blew forcibly.

'Don't go looking for problems. We've got enough as it is. As you'll find out, after one or two reconnaissance flights. The French coffee's good. Come and try some.'

The Mess was in a large tent in the middle of an orchard. This was Sergeant Karloff's idea, the apple trees camouflaging the tent from the air.

Triggers said, 'We've no idea, of course, if the Hun knows we're here yet. But if he does, then his machines will jolly soon be seeking out where his opposing team is operating from.'

'What about the canvas hangar though? He could spot that from several thousand feet.'

'Stop reminding me of all the things we haven't thought of,' Triggers snapped as they entered the Mess tent. Two packing crates served as tables. Triggers told MacEwen to 'pull up an ammunition box' and ordered two coffees from a Mess orderly who was washing the grime from his hands in a tin bowl. 'The poor devil's erected this tent four times in the last five days. As soon as we get settled and start to organize ourselves we're ordered to move on somewhere else. None of us know what's going on. We're given no specific orders. We fly out each day and report on whatever we think might be of value. Anyway, we've got a comfortable barn here with lots of clean straw. We've been sleeping under hedges for the last three nights. Thank God the weather's hot.'

'You mentioned a Sergeant Karloff. What's he – a Russian?' asked MacEwen.

'He's from Birmingham. And a splendid chap. They're all splendid, come to that. They can't have had more than a couple of hours' sleep since we arrived. Working day and night to keep us in the air on top of packing and unpacking with all this moving around. I just damn well hope they're working as hard back home to design some safer and faster machines for us.'

'Safer, maybe,' said MacEwen, thoughtful as he sipped his coffee. 'But not faster. Our role in this war is reconnaissance. So as far as the powers that be are concerned, the slower we fly the better. They won't care too much if we're shot to pieces as long as our information is accurate.'

'You Scots are a cunning lot,' Triggers said, flicking an earwig out of the sugar. 'And you're absolutely right, of course. In fact, there are many who'll find a deep satisfaction in the thought of us getting our fair share of the gunfire. I remember a chap in my old corps telling me that in the event of a war, transferring to the Flying Corps would be a coward's excuse for dodging the fighting.'

MacEwen asked after Bob Sears, Triggers's observer: had he managed to find his way to Amiens all right?

'Sick as a dog all the way, I'll bet,' MacEwen chuckled. 'He'd have been better off going back to his regiment, if you ask me.'

'Yes, he damn well would have been,' Triggers blazed in sudden anger. MacEwen looked taken aback. He had heard a lot about Triggers's unexpected outbursts but had never actually experienced one. Triggers stirred his coffee in silence for a moment. 'The poor devil caught one of those infantry bullets. He's in a pretty bad way.'

'Oh, I see. I'm sorry.'

'No need to be. Serves him damn well right. He would insist on me going down so he could take a closer look. The Squadron Commander is pressing for accurate information.'

At that moment the Duty Officer came urgently into the Mess to inform all present that they were wanted in the Squadron Commander's office immediately.

'We're on the move again, what d'you bet?' Triggers said impatiently, as they approached the ramshackle building that looked and smelled like a chickenhouse. Fortunately, there was so little room inside that the Squadron Commander suggested they should assemble outside. There was an air of suppressed excitement in his face as he stood before them.

'What we may have anticipated from our own reconnaissances in the past few days has now been confirmed,' he said. 'The British Army, dug in at this moment along the Condé canal, is planning to attack tomorrow morning.'

Triggers waited for the murmurs of approval to die down before voicing his doubt.

'In spite of the fact that on their right flank the French are falling back?'

The Squadron Commander looked at him for a moment, his face betraying nothing of his own opinion on the matter. He continued: 'Our job is to supply General Headquarters with accurate information regarding the movements of our own, the French and the enemy's forces and to report on anything else we think might be of interest. The strategies that arise from the study of such intelligence is not our concern.'

'But surely it should concern us if our reports are being ignored?' Triggers retorted.

'What do you mean by that?' the Squadron Commander barked. 'What reason have we to suggest that our reports are being ignored?'

'Two pilots in my Flight, sir, have reported long columns of German troops marching westwards along the Brussels–Ninove road. It's hard to believe GHQ could ignore that fact – plus the knowledge that the French are retiring on the right flank – and still insist on proceeding towards Mons.'

'Are you saying you have no faith in our Army to engage the enemy at Mons, Captain Triggers?'

There was an icy triumph in the Squadron Commander's tone. Triggers seethed in silence. What the hell could he say to that?

'And before we go questioning the judgement of GHQ,' the Squadron Commander went on, 'we'd better start questioning the veracity of our reconnaissance reports. Your observer, Sears, reported a column of enemy troops which turned out to be a stretch of black tarmacadam on an otherwise whitish road! Someone else reported a German encampment which was later found to be a field where the sheaves of corn were standing in rows. Now I know aerial reconnaissance is a difficult business, that we're all working under extremely trying conditions, and that the majority of you have been hastily trained. But we're not going to impress anyone – least of all, GHQ – with misleading information of that kind.' And he looked hard at Triggers before going on. 'So instead of moaning about GHQ mistrusting the information we're giving them – let's put our energies into making sure that they've no cause for mistrusting it.'

'I'm sorry if I spoke out of turn, sir,' Triggers said tersely.

The Squadron Commander acknowledged the apology with a curt nod.

'It's bloody confusion at the moment,' he said, giving rein to his own exasperation now. 'We all know that because we're in a position to see it all going on from up there. And if only we'd been properly trained and equipped during the past two years, instead of being baulked by dunderheads at every turn, we could have been a force to reckon with. As it is, we've now got to experiment and risk our despised skins in trial and error to find out our true worth – and to convince those who consider the Flying Corps to be no more than a useless bunch of smudge-faced mechanics that they can't win this damned war without us.'

He spoke this last sentence with a fervour that surprised himself as much as the assembled members of his Squadron, and, fumbling for his pipe, Triggers murmured 'hear hear'.

The battle of Mons began on the following morning. Soon after midday, the Squadron returned to the airfield to hand in their reconnaissance reports, to patch up their machines, refuel, and snatch a hasty lunch.

Triggers sat with his Flight in the Mess but ate nothing. He had seen too much of death that morning and the uselessness of his own role, flying up there in comparative safety above the gallant men of the British First Division who were being mercilessly shelled by German howitzers and remorselessly attacked by the hordes of von Kluck's infantry and three Divisions of cavalry, filled him with a paralysing rage. He dared not speak for fear of loosing the ferocious compassion he felt for the brave men whose lives might have been spared if only their commanders had believed the reports given into their hands by the RFC. The members of his Flight sensed all too well their leader's mood. They spoke quietly, careful not to address their conversation directly to him, and whenever he glared their way, they cut their conversations short.

'I must say our chaps are putting up a fight of it, in spite of the odds,' one of them said. 'Fifteen rounds per minute with those Lee-Enfield rifles. Lord, I thought they had machine guns on that first flight over the loop of the canal.'

'They haven't a chance though,' his observer replied. 'I don't understand why they haven't been ordered to retreat.'

Triggers rose abruptly from the table as the Mess orderly came up with the coffee on the lid of a tin which served as a tray.

'No time for that,' he muttered tersely. 'The poor devils being shot to pieces on the banks of the Condé have no time for coffee. Neither have we.'

He kicked an ammunition box savagely out of his way as he strode out. The others exchanged meaning glances and rose reluctantly from the table.

Out on the airfield the Squadron Commander was talking to a rigger who was examining the mainplanes of Triggers's Farman. Triggers ignored them both and climbed into the cockpit.

'She needs patching up,' the Squadron Commander said. He came over to Triggers and added, in a low voice, 'And it'll give you time to cool off a bit. It's at times like these we need to keep our heads, you know.'

'When everyone else is getting theirs blown off, you mean?'

The Squadron Commander looked steadily at him for a moment.

'This machine is unsafe to fly.'

'There's no novelty in that,' Triggers said and bawled at the mechanic to stop munching his disgusting-looking sandwich and swing the propeller.

Later that evening a cyclist arrived with a message from the field telephone tent and the Squadron assembled once again outside the 'chickenhouse'.

'It seems our reports are now believed,' the Squadron Commander said with a bitter smile. 'A bit late in the day, isn't it? The British Army is not going to attack, after all.'

'That's sensible,' Triggers muttered. 'Considering they're dying quite quickly enough where they are.'

'They're being asked to hold their position for twenty-four hours to enable Lanzerac's army to complete their move southwards.'

'To cover their retreat, you mean?' Triggers asked, with an innocent stare.

'I am conveying to you the message that was brought to me,' the Squadron Commander said pedantically. 'When the twenty-four hours are up, we'll be retreating ourselves, there's little doubt about that. Until that time we shall continue to fly and make our reports.'

The Squadron took off again at dawn. Triggers, with no replacement observer, flew alone, as he had done all the previous day. He turned north over Maubeuge and climbed to three thousand feet, looking down at the miles and miles of cultivated landscape, the differing greens of the fields of crops accentuated by the patches of brown furrowed earth: the industry of peace soon to be ravaged by warring armies once the retreat began. In the distance the guns were pounding and a pall of whitish smoke from the bursting shells hung over the Condé canal.

Triggers had not slept a wink all night or eaten since the previous morning's breakfast. At dinner the night before he had resisted the urge to accuse everyone present – including himself – of being cowards who had joined the Flying Corps to dodge the fighting. He was going insane with rage and frustration and there was nothing he could do about it. Here he was, flying at a safe height above the trajectory of the enemy shells, about to observe and report on the massacre of his countrymen. 10.20: Men being blown into the air; 10.30: Men being mown down by machine-gun fire; 10.50: Men being horribly mutilated. Is that what was expected of him? What the hell else was there to report in a situation like this? And it would be going on for another twelve hours or more yet. And he would be droning about up here, despised by his countrymen down there as a useless and spineless appendage with one bored eye on the carnage beneath him and the other on his fuel gauge, impatiently awaiting the time when his conscience would allow him to return to his airfield to enjoy a hot meal and warm his poor frozen fingers whilst theirs were engaged in the desperate game of kill or be killed.

He scanned the skies, begging for a Hun aeroplane to arrive upon the scene. He didn't know what he could do, armed as he was with only a Webley-Scott revolver, but at least he could put up some show of a fight to prove to them down there that at least he was as ready and willing to die as they were.

And he cursed himself for assuming that they were ready and willing to die; the poor devils were fighting like demons to keep the breath alive in their bodies. It was easy to be ready and willing to die when there wasn't much chance of death coming your way.

Angry tears burned his cheeks as he kicked viciously on the rudder-bar, turning south to fly back to the airfield. He was behaving like a bloody fool, he knew that. But there were times when being a bloody fool was the only thing that mattered.

'I've got my orders, sir,' the armoury sergeant said, taking the grenades from the box. 'It's six to each man.'

'Give me that box!'

'I'm sorry, sir, but—'

The sergeant reeled back as Triggers's fist caught him flush on the mouth. Triggers picked up the box of grenades and strode out.

In the air again, approaching the canal, he pushed the stick forward and entered the drifting cloud of smoke from the bursting high explosive shells. A shrill whistle followed by a vicious crump told him he was now in the path of the enemy gun trajectories and he could hear the fury of the British troops' Lee-Enfields as he dived low over the loop in the canal. Directly ahead he saw a wide field with a crop of spiked helmets and a forest of rifles pointing up at him. He kicked the left rudder, pulled the stick over, and the Farman went into a steeply banked turn as his right hand grabbed a grenade from the box. He gripped the ring with his teeth, drew the pin, and flung the grenade over the side. Then another, and another, as he roared low over the upturned faces and firing rifles, aware of a sound like fists being punched through tautened newspaper as bullets tore through the fabric of the mainplanes and the fuselage behind him. He shoved the stick forward, yelling in raucous delight at the sight of the sudden confusion of soldiers, stumbling, colliding, and flinging themselves to the ground. He flung three more grenades in rapid succession, then yanked on the stick as a house loomed ahead. She climbed steeply, and as he prayed she wouldn't stall he felt a sudden searing pain in his left shoulder. He'd been hit!

'I'm one of you now!' he shouted in fierce joy as he dived once again over the loop of the canal, southwards this time to where the British troops were dug in. And just before he turned to renew his lone attack, he saw a hand waving and imagined a welcoming shout from a comrade whose heart was warmed at the sight of the Union Jacks on the underside of the wings.

Oblivious of the shells screaming past, he turned once again towards the wide field of advancing German infantry, flying in even lower this time, turning across the field and flinging down grenades one after the other, and when the box was empty, he flung that down on them, too. He pulled on the stick as he approached the tall hedge between the house and the trees, laughing crazily at the tattered fabric of the mainplanes and thanking God for the Firth bullet-proof plate on which he was sitting; without it his behind would now be looking like a pepperpot.

As he rose above the tall hedge, the engine spluttered and coughed, the propeller blades clack-clacking ominously. He pushed the stick forward to maintain flying speed, his eyes intent on the field ahead.

She came down like a dream, stopping a dozen yards or so from the bank of the canal. A troop of Uhlans came galloping down the lane towards him. Triggers took the cartridge-shaped fusee canister from his pocket, ignited one of the matches and touched it to the fabric of the mainplanes. He made sure the fire was going nicely, then ran to the bank and dived into the cold waters of the canal. He surfaced, glanced back at the raging inferno, and, ignoring the pain in his left shoulder, swam to the waiting British troops on the opposite bank.

'Nice to see you wet instead of roasted alive,' the Corporal grinned as he hauled Triggers out. 'We thought you was burning along with her.'

Exhausted, Triggers sat on the bank and stared across the water. The flames had died but the black smoke was still rising. His teeth were chattering, yet the water had not been that cold. A chill had struck his heart at the Corporal's words. Was that to be his end? Instinctively, his right hand was drawn to the bulge in the pocket of his flying coat. Up there in the skies, the .45 Webley-Scott was a pretty futile means of self-defence. But, living with the constant threat of being 'roasted alive', it was a comforting thing for a man to have handy.

'We're waiting for the order to retreat,' the Corporal said. 'Gets my goat – having to give way to the Boche.'

Triggers agreed. But he didn't mind so much now. He had done his share. Pity about the Farman though. Still, she'd had her day. And at least she had burned alone.

chapter six

'I've you to thank for the interview, sir,' Alan said, wiping the greasy fingermarks from the bonnet of the Morris Oxford. 'If you hadn't written that letter to the War Office, I doubt they'd be seeing me on Monday.'

Colonel Starke had difficulty in hiding his concern. He had seen a good deal of the boy since Will Farmer's death. At first, he had felt a strong sense of responsibility for Alan's welfare inasmuch as his own son had been partly to blame for the tragedy. And his friendship with Alan helped to alleviate his bitter disappointment in his own son, Conway, who still continued to fritter his life away on useless inventions. He was now living in Farnborough, devoting his misdirected energies to a secret bomb that was to rid the British people of the terror of the Zeppelins by winging its way to those monstrous cigars and blowing them out of the skies. But all the bomb had done so far was to blow an enormous hole in the Colonel's bank balance.

Lonely in his retirement and with an ailing wife, the Colonel had grown to enjoy Alan's company. The boy rode well, was an excellent shot, and under the Colonel's expert instruction had become an accomplished swordsman, freely registering hits against a man who had been épée champion of his battalion in his younger days. Alan was extremely well coordinated, had an extraordinarily quick mind and was possessed of a calm indomitable spirit that was quite exceptional. The Colonel knew from his long experience of all kinds of men that Alan Farmer was made of the mettle of the truly brave. These qualities had been there all along, of course. The Colonel could hardly take the credit for what had been forged by four generations of Sussex blacksmiths. The question in the Colonel's mind was how much had he hardened and sharpened those qualities by taking such a strong hand in the boy's development? If he had not interfered, Alan might have looked upon the memory of his father's death as a warning; a terrible lesson learned. Instead of which – as far as the Colonel could make out – Alan appeared to regard the memory of that grim Saturday afternoon as a challenge. What other answer could there be when the boy was so keen to enlist for training in the Royal Flying Corps?

'Have you told your mother about this interview on Monday?' the Colonel enquired, somehow knowing what the answer would be.

'No.'

'Why not?'

'There's not much point in worrying her unnecessarily. They may not take me, you see.' Alan smiled ruefully. 'In fact, I'm pretty certain they won't.'

The Colonel tried his best to look put out. Not take him? After his own letter of recommendation to the War Office? Surely the Colonel's rank and service record counted for something?

'Your letter got me the interview, sir, but now it's up to me. And quite honestly, I haven't the qualifications. I'm a black-smith. Not even that yet. I haven't served my time, that is.'

Not that it made a whit of difference. A certificate from the National Master Farriers' Association was hardly likely to impress an interviewing officer looking for suitable candidates to train as fliers. They wanted young commissioned officers, chiefly from the cavalry.

'They take some civilians, surely?' asked the Colonel.

'Yes, sir. A few! Fellows from public schools and univer-sities.'

'A bit high-handed, aren't they? A Corps that has no tradi-tion, no battle honours?'

'They will have before the war's finished, sir,' Alan said proudly. 'After all, the first German defeat was brought about by military airmen.'

'Eh?'

'They spotted and reported von Kluck's swing-round to the

south-east from his march on Paris. So our Army was able to change its tactics accordingly.'

The Colonel nodded, recalling Alan's enthusiastic interest in military tactics, the long hours spent poring over books and maps and histories of famous battles, fathoming and arguing the generals' mistakes and brilliances that had lost or won the day. Alan had been particularly interested in the cavalry; not so much, oddly enough, in the stirring charges with sabre and lance, but in their duties as 'the eyes of the army', reconnoitring the movements of troops and supplies in an effort to divine the enemy's tactics by a diligent study of the deployment of their forces. The lad's interest now made sense to the Colonel and he realized that Alan's ambition to be a flier had been kindled quite some time ago. Indeed, the boy might well have had it in mind quite soon after his father's death; in which case the Colonel could take little or no credit for the boy's decision.

'About the radiator steaming,' Alan said, wrapping his tools into the rag spread out on the drive. 'It's the plugs. They're not really suitable for the Oxford. The makers recommend Bosch plugs. But as they're made in Germany . . .'

The Colonel agreed. Better a steaming radiator than helping to finance the enemy. Although, as an old soldier, he knew better than to believe the rumours of German atrocities that had prompted some of the more vindictive patriots in Becket's Hill to hurl insults at Arthur Borrowford's wife and stones at his pigs, all because the man had once boasted of a rich cousin who lived in Berlin. The Colonel had set about the 'patriots' with his walking-stick.

'You'll find she won't skid if you put the foot-brake and the hand-brake on lightly together, sir.' Alan wiped the offending splashes of mud from the acetylene headlamp, reminded the Colonel that the rear oil lamps needed topping up and silently prayed that the old man never ventured out in the Oxford after dusk. He had seen him negotiating the series of sharp bends leading down to Lovell's Bridge and feared for the old man's life. But no more than the Colonel feared for Alan's.

'How any young chap could want to sit up there in the sky

with everything on the ground letting fly at him and with no means of retaliation, is absolutely beyond me. You're no more than a sitting duck. At the mercy of everything and everyone. Most of all from your own mount.' He had heard from some engine fitter chap with disgusting fingernails about the constant engine troubles, bits falling off machines at the most inconvenient moments, and quite hair-raising tales of unexpected and totally unaccountable antics, as if the thing had suddenly taken on a life of its own in a determined effort to extinguish that of its rider. The flying machine was menace enough to any chap fool enough to fly one in peacetime without all the added hazards of war. By the time the next war came around they might have perfected the damned thing but it was sheer nonsense to go talking about it as if it had already replaced the horse. Oh yes, he agreed that horses got stuck in the Flanders mud. But so did everything else. So had the war, come to that. But a horse you could depend on, at least. Faithful to the last breath. She would be there between your legs until her own were shot from under her. But a flying machine ... it was going willingly hand-in-glove with a murderous traitor.

Alan made no reply as he packed his tools into the wooden box on the rack of his motor bicycle. The Colonel wished he had kept his mouth shut. Dammit, the young man wanted to enlist as thousands of other young men were doing all over the country. He was offering his life in the service of his King and the Empire, and, if God chose, he would die a noble death in the pursuance of his duty. In the event of such a tragedy, would it be of any importance at all if the lad died in the air or on the ground? Either way, his mother's grief would be the same.

'Will you be going out shooting on Saturday, sir?'

The Colonel was undecided. There was something shameful about shooting pheasants and partridges when your regiment was 'over there' engaged in much grimmer sport. Alan understood and did his best to ease the Colonel's mind by suggesting the bag be sent to the new open-air hospital, where the game birds would surely be relished by fellows who had eaten nothing but bully beef for months on end. And the shoot could hardly be termed a sport this year. No, it was more a duty. There had been so little shooting with the bad winter floods that the birds had flourished unchecked, and now, having fed well on the fruits of the previous mild autumn and their morale encouraged by their unthinned ranks, they were preparing to attack the new seed to be sown now the floods had cleared up.

The Colonel had to smile. Alan made it sound like a war in which the Colonel was the commanding saviour of the seed, protecting it from a ravaging enemy. But there, it was he who had trained the boy to think like a soldier.

'Very well, Alan, you've convinced me that a shoot would be doing my bit. And I wish you well at your interview on Monday.'

'Thank you, sir. I think I shall need it.'

'Oh – and do remember me to your Uncle Albert.'

Alan reminded him once again that his name was 'Harry'.

'Ah yes, of course. Harry! Invalided out, eh? Must be a bad wound.'

As Alan passed through the booking hall the woman behind the grille gave him a friendly smile. Rather too friendly, Alan thought. Surely she didn't think he was meeting trains on the pretext of seeing her? After all, she must have been at least as old as his mother.

After taking ten minutes to start his motor cycle, Alan blessed Uncle Harry, wounded or not, for neglecting to say in his letter what time of day he would be coming. Riding back to Becket's Hill he thought clearly about all the irritations of the past few days and came to the conclusion that they stemmed from the guilt he was feeling for not having yet told his mother about the interview at the War Office on Monday. Why did she have to make it so difficult for him? Surely she must have seen the poster on the wall of the post office? You could hardly miss it. 'Women of Britain say GO!' Why couldn't she pat him proudly on the back and say 'Go and good luck!' like all the other mothers and wives?

As he turned into Haverton Lane a batch of new recruits were marching along. Farm labourers mostly; corduroys and flannel shirts, the earth still on their boots, doing their best to stiffen back shoulders bent from ploughing. They looked cheerful enough despite the wicked-faced sergeant who herded them along complaining that they looked about as smart as a row of newly dug potatoes. And why shouldn't they look cheerful? *Their* mothers had obviously patted them on the back and told them what 'splendid fellows' they were.

'Kitchener's New Army'. Watching at the smithy door, old Tom cast a critical eye after the marching shambles. 'No uniforms and broomhandles to fight with.'

'A new broom sweeps clean,' Sam Herbert said, philosophically. 'Though whether they'll do as good a job on the fields o' France as they do home here, I wouldn't like to say.'

And they went back into the smithy where Percy, the apprentice, had been damping down the dust with the sprinkling can and was clouted round the ear for turning the place into a pond.

Alan lingered outside, glancing up at the signboard over the open double doors. 'W. Farmer. Shoeing and General Smith'. When he had finished his apprenticeship it would be changed to 'A. Farmer'. According to his mother, that time was not so far away. It was a shame to disappoint her, Alan thought, but if they turned him down for training as a flier at the interview on Monday he decided he would take the King's shilling and a broomhandle and join the row of newly dug potatoes shuffling around the corner into Leadby Street.

'Harry not on that one either, eh?' Old Tom wiped the sweat from his face in the towel that hung on the string over the forge. 'What time's the next?'

'Quarter past one.'

'Perhaps he'll be on that one.'

'Perhaps,' Alan said, impatiently. 'You shrunk the new tyres on Collins's cart yet?'

No, Tom had not. He hadn't even made the tyres yet. Jobs had to take their turn and never mind who the customer was. You couldn't hurry jobs like that. That was the trouble with the young ones today; all rush and tear and rough ends. Proper work took time and care.

'And it's Collins we're putting those tyres on for. Not his slip of a daughter.'

Alan turned away, his face reddening. Tom grinned.

'Lorna Collins, I know, I got eyes. Well, well! Have you told her yet? That you're joining up, I mean?'

Alan glanced uneasily around, afraid that the others might have heard.

'I'm not joining up. It's an interview, that's all. I've told you that. And no one else knows. You know that, too.'

'What about the Colonel?'

'I'm not counting the Colonel.'

'I suppose he thinks you should be an officer, eh?'

Alan was silent for a moment.

'The Colonel's against it. He hasn't said as much but I know he doesn't want me to join the Flying Corps.'

'I shouldn't think your mother will either,' Tom said. And there was a faint look of disdain on his face. 'You haven't told her yet then?'

'No. I haven't.'

'High time she knew, don't you think? Friday! And the interview on Monday.'

There was a hard warning gleam in Alan's eye.

'I'll be the one to tell her,' he said, moving to the yard. 'No one else.'

Tom snatched the shovel from the apprentice, who was stoking the forge as if he was articled to the Devil.

'Here, young 'un! There's a war on! That coal costs!'

The boy ducked instinctively as Tom tossed the shovel on to the coal box.

'That Alan,' he hissed, glaring into the flames where the fresh coal was burning. 'The damn young fool! You'd have thought he'd have learned his lesson, seeing what happened to his father.'

*

Molly was looking at her hair in the small oval mirror near the kitchen range when Alan came in. She was wearing a new skirt. At least, he thought it was new.

'Three years old this is,' she said, pleased with her reflection. 'Made it from a pattern. He wasn't on the twelve o'clock train then? The dinner'll be cooked away to nothing.' She moved the simmering pots on the range. 'He'll think I'm an awful cook. They put the new tyres on Collins's cart yet?'

'No! Lightning, Tom is. You can't hurry him. There's a war on. His favourite saying these days. Keeps 'em all at bay.'

'Over by Christmas they said. And here we are end of February. Have you seen what they're paying for the mule and horseshoes on that War Office contract? I'm not at all sure we should take it on.'

Alan was inclined to agree, especially with Old Tom making every shoe as if it were going on the horse of a General. He watched his mother fiddling with her hair again and thought of Wilf Sillett. Just before Christmas, Sillett had bought one of the new Ivel tractors with a high chassis to keep the gears free from soil and stones. It had failed to start one morning and Alan went over to Sillett's farm to take a look. As he was taking his tools from the rack on his motor bike he heard Sillett talking to one of his labourers in the barn.

'A beautiful little piece she is. I wouldn't mind at all, given half a chance. And a widow, too, so she'd be hot for it, no doubt.' The labourer had agreed and said he wouldn't mind a turn himself when Sillett had finished with her. Alan had a strong suspicion that they were talking about his mother and when Sillett turned up at the smithy a few days later Alan watched him like a hawk. Sillett had hung about in the yard while they were shoeing his horses, his eyes continually glancing at the back door of the house, and he looked sorely disappointed when he left without having seen her. Alan had waited until he reached the end of Leadby Street before he caught him up.

'Keep your eyes from my mother in future,' he said. He was ready for Sillett's punch and evaded it quite easily. He caught Sillett by the throat with his left hand, the smith's 'tongs hand' as Tom called it, reckoning the grip became so strong that the tips of the fingers could meet the thumb even at the throat of a bull. 'You're as slow as your animals as well as thinking like them. Keep your eyes from my mother. Understand?'

'I won't be told what to do by a bloody boy,' Sillett said in a strangled voice, struggling to free himself from the iron grip.

'It's not a boy's hand that's holding you,' Alan said with an icy calm. 'And it won't let go until you promise not to see or speak of my mother again.'

'You're a madman,' Sillett said, after he had promised. 'And you'll pay for this, my lad, don't think you won't.'

'You're a hooligan,' Molly told Alan when she had heard from Tom that they had lost one of their best customers. 'Sillett's still got the bruises on his neck, they say. And what for? What was it all over? Anyway, he's taking his horses to Hopford to be shod from now on. A fine thing! Between you and the Army purchasing officer buying up all the horses, we'll be tinkers on the road soon, looking for a living.'

Alan had never thought of his mother as a 'desirable woman' before the Sillett episode. Since then, he had been more alert whenever his mother was being discussed, and he had noticed a different light in the Colonel's eyes in recent weeks; what had once been a light of concern for the 'brave little woman' was now bright and enquiring when he asked after 'that young lady, your mother'. It was as if he was expecting news from Alan of another man in the offing. And he quite often made allusions to her beauty, referring to something or other as being of 'a rather deeper gold than your mother's hair' or making a casual mention of the colour of her eyes in an attempt to describe the glorious waters he had sailed in some overcrowded troopship.

Watching his mother closely in recent weeks, Alan was acutely aware of the changes in her appearance and behaviour. Gone were the dark shadows that had seemed to deepen whenever she looked at the small photograph in the mahogany frame on the mantel. She no longer sat for hours on end in front of the range staring into the flames and then wondering where the time had gone. She sang about the house, ran upstairs, slammed doors instead of closing them as if afraid of disturbing the dead.

'If his cart won't be ready we ought to let Arthur Collins know,' Molly said. 'He did say he'd call for it at two.'

'I've told him. I called at the farm.' And he opened his new copy of *Flight* and waited for the question she was sure to ask.

'Did you see Lorna?'

Alan looked as if he had never heard of the girl. No, he hadn't seen her, he lied, his voice somewhere down in his boots. In fact, Lorna's father had told him that she was over with the pigs and Alan had gone the long way round past the pigsty in the hope of seeing her. Then wished he hadn't bothered; he had never seen a girl in such muck.

'She's grown into a nice girl. Hard to think she was that awkward little creature in your class at Lovell's school.'

Alan flicked the pages of *Flight* in an effort to hide his indignation. Awkward, indeed? She was the most graceful creature ever born.

'She was telling me she'll have to do the milk round now that Albert Warren's joined up.'

'Women doing all sorts now,' Alan said, looking at the new pusher biplane that was 'sure to win the admiration of the gallant British airmen at the Front' and wishing that someone would pass a law against slave-driving farmers who used the war as an excuse to work their gentle, sweet, loving daughters to death. 'There was a woman in the booking office at the station this morning.'

'And they're coming out of Claybourne's factory in Caxton just like men. Cigarettes, hands as black as the devil's and language all colours, they say.'

She shook her head, utterly bewildered by it all. The war was a mystery to her. She couldn't understand why it had to be; why everyone was so enthusiastic about it, talking of nothing but the 'bit' they were 'doing' to keep it going. It was as if life would come to a stop if their daily contribution to death ceased to be. She didn't want to think about the war. Now that she had put the grey world of grief behind her she wanted only to enjoy the brightness of living. Thank God the war was 'over there' and she could put it from her mind for most of the time despite all the talk of it.

'Another aeroplane book?'

'This week's!'

'Isn't it time you found yourself another interest?'

He knew better than to ask 'what', but she told him just the same.

'The poor girl's running out of excuses for coming here. She's brought me so many eggs I've got a cupboard full there. At least you could ask her to tea.'

'Caught a Blighty wound,' Alan said, to change the subject. 'Uncle Harry! But he didn't say what, or where.'

'Can't say much in eight lines, can you? Eight lines! And three years almost since we saw him last. Your father's funeral. And eleven years before that.' And she sighed as if it was all a bit of a bother to her. 'A good job we hung on to that old bed or we'd have nowhere for him to sleep.'

'You think he'll stay then?'

'How do I know? He won't stay long, knowing Harry. But he'll have to stay tonight, at least. He can't get to Wiltshire tonight, can he?'

'Is that where he'll be going?'

'That's where he was living the last time he wrote, when he told us they'd sent for him to join his regiment.' Again she sighed. 'If only he'd written to say he was wounded we could have gone to the hospital to see him.'

And that would have saved him coming to the smithy; that's what she meant, Alan thought. Harry was bringing the war too close to home for her comfort, of course.

'Are Luke Evans's shovels ready?' Molly asked. The shovels were, but no handles, Alan told her. 'Luke will flay me. I said they'd be done if he called this afternoon. What'll I tell him?'

'That our carpenter's on the square in Caxton. Marching up and down with half a uniform and a rifle he made himself on the bench out there.'

No broomhandle for him, Ted May had said. If it had to be a wooden rifle then at least it would look like one. He had made the wooden tool-box to fit on the rack of Alan's Lea

Francis; also pipe-holders for Tom and Sam, and a cricket bat for young Percy, handing them out on his last day in the smithy, with apologies all round for leaving them short-handed.

'A fool Ted was, joining up like that.'

'His wife says she's proud of him,' Alan said. She was looking in the mirror again and he thought this might be the moment to break the news of the interview on Monday. 'Women of Britain say go.'

'What?'

'It's a poster on the wall of the post office.'

'It's that Miss Edwards,' she said, looking at her tongue in the mirror to make sure that was beautiful, too. 'Chivvying all the men to join up. It's all very well for her. She doesn't have a man in the house.' And she gave a little rueful smile. 'Call the kettle black!'

Alan was still fuming when he reached the rise on the other side of Lovell's Bridge. No man in the house, indeed. He was eighteen years old. Chaps his age were already up to their necks in glory in the trenches. He stopped on Lovell's Bridge and watched the dwindling reminder of the winter floods and wished his mother would flow with the tide. 'The war has to be fought,' he murmured to the running waters. 'Men have to go. And I am a man. So I must go.'

The Union Jack, ragged and damp, hung limply on two tired lengths of string from Miss Edwards's bedroom window. She was leaning on the gate as Alan roared past; a bunch of white feathers and a crabbed old face, looking out for anything in civilian trousers – or knickerbockers, come to that. Alan smiled as he remembered Charlie Rampling swearing at her when she had all but blinded him with the biggest feather in the bunch. 'Can't you see what's up here?' Charlie had raged. 'Industrial Army badge! To save me the taunts of the likes of you. And have you never heard of age limits? Christ Almighty, woman, I've got four grandchildren. It's you they should put in a trench. And fill the damn thing in.'

Alan gave her a friendly wave, slowed down to explain that she had already given him three white feathers, commented on the weather, and thoroughly agreed with her look of disdain.

If only his mother had just a spoonful of Miss Edwards's fervour, he thought, as he took the right fork instead of carrying straight on to the station. It was twenty minutes before Uncle Harry's train was due in – if he was on the train, that is – and if he rode past Collins's farm he might catch a glimpse of the graceful, gentle creature. His mother was right, of course. He should ask the girl to tea. He should have asked her long ago. But he always got so damned tongue-tied when he was in her presence. It was stupid really because he'd known the girl as long as he could remember.

There was no sign of Lorna as he rode past the farm. And he really had made up his mind to ask her to tea on Sunday. Damn the girl! And his mother! Women did make life difficult for a man.

chapter seven

The guard unrolled his green flag and was preparing to blow his whistle when Harry, dressed in hospital blue and with a kitbag on his shoulder, strode on to the platform. The nurse, flushed and breathless and half regretting her stop at the book-stall to buy a magazine, heaved the suitcase from one hand to the other, glancing at the painful weal across her fingers. The suitcase had one hinge missing, two rusted catches that did not work, and was dubiously secured with a length of fraying string, which also served as a handle. A less forbearing young woman might have asked why the dickens Harry Farmer insisted on hanging on to a so-called article of luggage at which any discerning tramp might have turned up his nose. Harry had bought the suitcase for that holiday in Brighton almost twenty years ago and as far as he was concerned, it still served its purpose, and was quite good enough to go knocking about on the tops of wardrobes in back-bedroom lodgings.

'Hurry along there, please!' The guard flapped his flag im-patiently against his knee, then, becoming aware of Harry's disability, he moved briskly and importantly along the plat-form to the second coach, holding up a hand as if to say 'just leave it to me'. 'Here we are, Tommy Atkins.' He turned the shining brass handle and gave Harry a kindly wink. 'First Class for you, eh?'

There were two women in the compartment. One of them glared at the guard and looked crossly at the kitbag as it thumped on her feet.

'Beg your pardon, madam,' Harry murmured and took the suitcase from the nurse.

'Are you sure you can manage now?'

'Yes, thank you, nurse.'

'And there will be someone waiting to meet you at Becket's Hill?'

Yes, there would be. The guard's whistle blew. Harry thanked her for the magazine and made a little awkward wave with it as the train drew away. Then he pulled up the window; the signal for the two women to look down at their books again.

Harry looked at his suitcase and kitbag, then up at the luggage racks. There was plenty of room if the parcels were rearranged; it was simply a matter of asking the ladies' permission. But he had no right to be in a First Class compartment and although he had lived with his disability for six weeks now he was still hesitant about drawing attention to himself; particularly the attention of two such finely dressed ladies of the upper class.

'I beg your pardon. Would you ladies mind if I moved—'

'Oh, I'm so sorry,' one of them said, jumping up. 'How stupid of me. I didn't think.'

'No, I can move mine,' said the other. 'They're smaller.'

Harry leaned stiffly back as they jostled and bustled in the swaying compartment.

'Here, put this one of mine on top of yours.'

'Yes, that's better. Put this one over there.'

'Mind the hats! There we are. Now! The suitcase!'

'That's quite heavy,' Harry protested. 'And I can manage—'

But the suitcase had already been hoisted on to the rack.

'What about the kitbag?'

'It can stay just where it is. It's in no one's way. And if someone else comes in they'll jolly well have to put up with it.'

And they stood there smiling at Harry, happy at having been of some assistance and grateful for the activity which had cleared the air of embarrassment and enabled them to look at him as if there was nothing so very unusual about him, after all.

Women were such gentle, sympathetic creatures, Harry thought, as he settled in the corner seat with his magazine. Even these upper class ladies in their finery were no different from the rest, despite their knifing voices. And he mused on an artist's impression of the fighting north of Soissons and thought the picture heroically at odds with the war as he had experienced it. Over the page, in the 'Dead on the Field of Honour', his eyes were drawn by some mysterious guiding finger to a face that he recalled, and he wondered what the man's wife would be feeling at this moment.

Later, as he gazed through the carriage window at the smooth rounded slopes of the Downs, he thanked God that he had never married. He could suffer any amount of pain. But the pain in a wife's eyes at the sight of his empty left sleeve ... that would have been too much to bear.

When the train arrived at Becket's Hill, Harry leaned out of the compartment window and Alan ran up to greet him.

'I hardly recognized you,' Harry grinned. 'You've grown a bit.'

'It's three years,' Alan said, suddenly aware of the pinned-up left sleeve as Harry handed him the suitcase. 'We got your letter. If we'd known you were in hospital we could have come to see you.'

The two ladies wished Harry well and waved from the window as the train pulled away. Harry asked after Alan's mother as they walked to the motor bike parked by the hedge.

'She's well enough,' Alan said, wondering how she would look when she saw the man's pinned-up left sleeve.

'No sense in pushing that heavy machine when you can be riding,' Harry said when they had strapped the suitcase and the kitbag on to the rack of the motor bike. 'You've lightened my load. So off you go. I shall enjoy the walk. Looking at all the old familiar sights.'

Alan started his bike and rode off. As he approached the bend in the road, he glanced back at the lone striding figure. Harry waved cheerily and Alan pondered on his uncle's plight as he rode on through the scanty colours of a February countryside. Harry was a blacksmith; a craftsman whose living depended on the skill in his two hands.

'Fancy that,' Molly said when Alan told her. And she sank into the armchair by the range. 'Which arm is it?'

'The left one.'

Molly nodded and stared into the fire.

'He wouldn't take the omnibus,' Alan went on. 'He wanted to walk. I think he wanted me to be here first, so I could tell you. I expect he thought it would ease the shock.'

'He's a strange boy,' Molly said, her voice barely audible. Then she gave a short hard laugh. 'Boy, indeed? But there – I can't be expected to think of him as a man. We've only seen him twice since he left here all those years ago.'

'He seemed more concerned about the pocket watch than his arm.'

'Pocket watch?'

'Dad's! I gave it to Uncle Harry when he came to the funeral.'

Harry had explained that if only he had kept the watch in his right-hand breast pocket instead of the left one, it might have been unaffected. As it was, the watch had been shattered during the incident in which he had lost his left arm.

'I'll go and meet him,' Alan said. 'It'll be company for the rest of the way.'

When Alan had gone, Molly sat there for a long time looking at the other armchair and thinking of those evenings long ago, with Harry sitting there in his best trousers and clean shirt, his face scrubbed and shining, his hair brushed and carefully parted. She felt strangely guilty. If she had not come to the house as Will's wife, would Harry have left Becket's Hill as he had done to join the Army? She thought not. It was her fault he had lost an arm.

Then her guilt was replaced by annoyance at his coming there. He had not shown his face all these years, apart from attending his brother's funeral, so why had he chosen to pay a visit to them now? Was he coming to make her suffer? Hadn't she suffered enough since Will's death? His coming would open closed doors, revive old memories, and resurrect the grief she had suffered and put behind her. Damn the man for coming now. He'd have to stay the night, of course. It was too late for him to travel on to wherever it was he was going. If only he could come and go without her seeing him.

And in a panic at the thought of him crossing the yard to the back door, she ran upstairs and dried her eyes. Then she stood at the window and watched him walking down the lane with Alan. And she wept again; this time out of pity for the man, vexation at her selfishness, and anger at the men responsible for the war and its cruelties.

'Well, Harry, you look fit enough, bully beef or no,' Old Tom said, the warmth in his eyes concealing any pain he felt at the sight of the pinned-up sleeve. 'You'll be staying a while, I hope?'

'Shrinking on a new cart tyre, I see,' Harry said, evading the question. 'And another in the oven, eh?'

'For Arthur Collins,' Alan explained. 'He's coming round at two.'

'If it's not done, he'll have to wait,' Tom said truculently. And he turned to Harry. 'All rush and tear, this one. Mechanics we would have been now, if he'd had his way. Wanted to turn us into a garage. A pump outside if the war hadn't come. Motor cars coming for miles to fill up.'

'We have to move with the times,' Alan said quietly.

'Move, maybe!' Tom snapped. 'But not rush headlong. Your father found out the folly of that.'

Harry caught the angry spark in Alan's eyes and tactfully brought the conversation back to the heating cart tyre.

'Don't let me hold you up,' he said. 'That tyre looks just about ready.'

It was heated to its full expansion and all hands were given to the task of 'shrinking on'. The wheel was laid flat upon the wooden stand, Alan taking four old rasps from the carpenter's shop and driving them lightly in around the circumference. Whilst Sam and Old Tom accomplished the ticklish job of removing the red-hot tyre from the oven, Harry and the apprentice filled the buckets with water for the shrinking.

'What's it like at the Front, sir?' the apprentice enquired of the one-armed hero who had enlivened the dull air of the smithy with the sound of bursting shells. 'Did you shoot a lot of Germans?'

'I shod a lot of horses,' Harry grinned. 'We were short of farriers.'

The boy looked sorely disappointed.

'Hurry up with that water,' Old Tom called urgently, as they laid the red-hot rim carefully over the wheel so as not to burn the wood. 'Right, Alan!'

Alan knocked out the supporting rasps and the rim fell into position around the circumference of the wheel.

'Pour it on!' Old Tom ordered as Harry came up with the bucket. 'Quick now, or she won't shrink on true.'

Alan glared at Old Tom. The insensitive old fool should have realized that Harry was doing his best to help but couldn't be expected to manage the pouring with one arm. Alan thanked his uncle, took the bucket and poured the water over the red-hot rim.

Unnoticed by the men, Molly stood in the smithy doorway, the hissing clouds of steam casting her mind back to the kettle of water spilling over the fire in the hazel coppice when Harry had punched the bodger to the ground for daring to put a hand on her. And she compared the fierce confidence and carefree independence of the young man he had been to the man she saw now, looking on in helpless inactivity at the busy hands of the other men.

'I saw you from the window,' she called. 'I've been waiting in the kitchen.'

Harry gazed at her, not knowing what to say. She looked more beautiful than ever, he thought.

'The dinner's all ready on the table,' she went on. 'I thought you'd be hungry after your journey.' The line of washing was blowing in the wind as they crossed the yard. 'The pulley you made me to haul up the line. It's still working, you see.'

'Did you see many BE2s at the Front?' Alan enquired as they sat down to eat.

'We couldn't tell one aeroplane from another,' Harry said

with a faint smile. 'But we didn't look too hard, I suppose. If they were high you didn't bother. If they were low enough – well – you shot at them.'

Alan looked shocked.

'Without knowing which side they were on?'

'Some reckoned none of 'em were on our side. Up there in the clean sky – and off to a warm bed and a hot meal. They're officers, you see. Transferred from the cavalry.'

'Not all of them,' Alan said, and feeling his mother's gaze, looked down at his plate. 'They're taking civilians now.'

'Aye,' Harry said. 'If they're off the train from Eton.'

Old Tom put his head around the door.

'Lorna Collins has called for the cart.'

Alan reddened, tried his best to look annoyed, put his dinner in the oven to keep warm and went out to the smithy.

'They were in the same class in school,' Molly explained, smilingly. 'She keeps making excuses for calling here. But Alan thinks of nothing but aeroplanes.'

Harry sensed her concern. They ate in silence for a time.

'I wrote to you about a month after you came to Will's funeral,' Molly said. 'But the letter was returned.'

'I moved around a lot after I left the Regular Army. Six or seven jobs.'

'As blacksmith?'

'Aye.'

He was having trouble cutting the beef. Molly took his plate.

'It's a bit on the tough side,' she said lightly, taking his knife and fork and cutting the meat. 'What will you do – now, I mean?'

'I haven't made up my mind yet.'

'You're welcome to stay.'

Harry said nothing. She sensed his reluctance.

'Till you've decided what you want to do, I mean,' she said, handing him his plate. Then, after a long silence in which they searched desperately for something to say, she gave a little laugh. 'The coming thing, Will used to say. We'd all be flying soon and thinking nothing of it.'

*

'One of the felloes on the wheel needed looking at,' Alan said with an air of importance. 'But we won't charge your father for that.'

Lorna thanked him in a quiet voice and Alan was acutely aware of her nearness as he made out the bill on the end of the carpenter's bench.

'You're taking on the milk round then?'

'Yes. So I shall get around the village now. Meet people. It can be a bit lonely working on the farm.'

'I daresay,' Alan said as he handed her the bill. 'Can you manage the cart? Or should I come part of the way – yes, I'd better, just to see that new tyre's on proper.'

He helped her on to the cart and climbed up beside her. Old Tom came into the smithy doorway and grinned up at them.

'Two to manage one horse, eh?'

'We're getting behind with the shoes for that Army contract,' Alan said, taking the reins as if the fate of the British cavalry were in his young brown hands. 'So carry on with them till I get back.'

'Young show-off,' Tom growled as the cart rumbled off down the lane.

They sat in silence all the way to Lovell's Bridge, both looking around at the countryside as if they had never seen it before.

'My Uncle Harry's been invalided out,' Alan said, as they crossed the bridge. 'He's had a lot of interesting experiences, no doubt. Perhaps – well – you might like to hear them. In which case – you might like to come to tea on Sunday. That is – if you're not otherwise engaged.'

Molly was making the tea for the men in the smithy when Lorna knocked on the back door. Molly smiled inwardly and wondered what the girl's excuse would be this time. It was a message for Alan from Colonel Starke. He would drive Alan to the station on Monday if Alan would let him know the time of the train. Molly looked bewildered.

'Alan's not going anywhere on Monday.'

'Oh. The Colonel seemed to think he was going up to London.'

'London?' Molly laughed. 'Whatever would Alan be going to London for?'

Lorna had an uneasy feeling that she should have taken the message directly to Alan.

'I expect the Colonel got it wrong,' she said. 'I'll be going then.'

They almost collided in the doorway and Alan's eyes lit up with pleasure on seeing her.

'She's brought a message for you,' Molly explained. 'Colonel Starke seems to think you're going up to London on Monday.'

Alan avoided his mother's enquiring gaze and poured the tea into the cups on the tray.

'Old Tom's dying of thirst out there,' he said. 'That's right! I am going to London. I've got an interview at the War Office.'

Molly stared at him for a time. Alan turned to face her.

'I'm sorry I didn't tell you before,' he said. 'But there wasn't a lot of point. It's very likely I won't be suitable.'

'Suitable for what?'

'Training as a pilot in the Royal Flying Corps.'

Molly sank into the armchair.

'I knew there was something in the wind,' she said in a low voice. 'But I had no idea it was that.'

Lorna looked uncomfortable and apologized for causing trouble. Alan reassured the stricken girl and reminded her that she had promised to come to tea on the following afternoon.

'A fine thing,' Molly said, when Lorna had gone. 'My son joining up and not telling me.'

'I'm not joining up. I've told you. It's an interview, that's all. And I wouldn't have got that far if Colonel Starke hadn't written a letter of recommendation.'

That was quite enough for Molly. If Colonel Starke had written on Alan's behalf then her son was as good as in uniform.

'I understand how it is for you,' she said, her eyes flickering towards the photograph of Alan's father. 'And I know that men have to go. I wish I could be like others and say go and good luck, but . . .' She hung her head.

Alan tried to comfort her but she pushed him away and sharply told him not to fuss. Alan sighed impatiently and picked up the tray.

'Even Harry says I haven't got the proper qualifications,' he said. Molly asked about the letter from the War Office. 'It's only one of those dear sir your obedient servant letters. It's not signed by the King or anything.'

'Don't joke,' she said tartly, 'I'd like to see it all the same.'

Alan plonked down the tea tray and moved to the stairs.

'If you're worried about the smithy,' he said, 'the place runs itself. If they did accept me – well – it's only a matter of you finding another man.'

'Plenty of them about, of course,' she snapped.

Alan clenched his teeth and ran up the stairs.

'And fetch your suit while you're up there,' Molly called after him. 'It'll need a press for London.'

chapter eight

When Alan entered the War Office waiting room, a young man with a wispy moustache was talking to a very tall young cavalry officer.

'I thought it would make me look older,' Wispy Moustache said. 'But you have to be eighteen for a commission. So the Royal Flying Corps is my only chance now. They *want* younger chaps.'

'You need to be seventeen, though,' the cavalry officer said.

Wispy Moustache looked offended.

'I *am* seventeen. Well – I shall be in August. You'll have no trouble getting in, of course. Transferring from the cavalry. If you can ride a horse, you can fly an aeroplane. That's what they say.'

The door of the interview room opened and a dejected young man in civilian clothes came out. Wispy Moustache swallowed nervously and rapped on the door. 'Come in,' a voice boomed. Wispy Moustache assumed a confident air and went in.

'I suppose you thought the same,' the cavalry officer said to Alan. 'Your own marvellous idea. Then you find half the chaps in the country want to be fliers.' Alan smiled his agreement. 'You're not one already, by any chance?'

'No,' Alan said. 'But I used to think I was. When I was fifteen. A friend of my father had a machine they'd rebuilt. I used to sit in it for hours, working the controls. And they let me taxi her.'

'But you didn't actually fly it?'

'I took her a few feet off the ground once. My father skinned me alive.'

'Wouldn't they let you fly her later on? When you were older, I mean?'

'My father crashed her. He was killed.'

'Oh.'

They sat in silence for a time. Then the cavalry officer introduced himself.

'I'm Charles Gaylion, by the way.'

'Alan Farmer.'

Wispy Moustache came out of the interview room. He had not been accepted. There was nothing left for him now but to go back to school.

'Trouble is, we're at the wrong end of the day,' he said. 'He must have seen forty or fifty chaps today and he's as irritable as hell.'

And true enough, Major Lanchester was not in the best of moods, Charles Gaylion thought as he stood before him.

'There are chaps who can – and chaps who can't,' Major Lanchester snapped. 'And most of you can't. Believe me!'

'But I know I can fly an aeroplane, sir,' Charles said, exuding the total confidence that he knew was expected of a candidate at such interviews.

'Of course you do,' said Major Lanchester. Confidence alone was not enough; he had seen too many young men crashing precious machines with all the confidence in the world. 'But we haven't the machines or the time to give everyone a shot at it.'

'I play rather a lot of tennis, sir. I understand that's important.'

'Yes, it is. Lancers, eh? So I shan't ask you if you can ride a horse.'

'Might as well ask if I can walk, sir.'

'Are you a good soldier, Gaylion?'

'Yes, I am, sir,' Charles replied, rather too emphatically.

'Someone who might disagree?'

Charles was loyally silent. The Major smiled faintly.

'Your CO perhaps? Doesn't want you to transfer, eh? I know. Nasty, smelly things, aeroplanes. Hardly suitable conveyances for gentlemen. What's your opinion, Gaylion?'

'No one loves horses more than I do, sir. But – well – the war as it is – two wings in the air are rather more efficient than four hooves in the mud.'

The Major smiled appreciatively and Charles felt he was already sitting in the cockpit of a Farman 'Longhorn' training machine.

'Well, Gaylion. You seem to have all the right qualifications.'

'Thank you, sir.'

'Question is – have you also got all the wrong ones?'

Charles could hardly believe his ears. Surely the Major wasn't going to turn him down?

'I'm afraid I don't understand, sir.'

'Neither do I. But an awful lot of chaps like you turn out to be duds and are sent back to their regiments. How are you mechanically?'

Charles blinked.

'Don't the troops do all that, sir?'

'What if you're forced down over enemy lines? The 'troops' will all be Huns.'

'I see what you mean, sir. Well, sir, if it's a matter of reading it up . . .'

'It's a matter of getting some grease on your hands. Stand up, will you?'

'I know what you're thinking, sir. But I've actually sat in one and there was heaps of room.'

The Major looked uncertainly up at the tall figure. Charles now exuded anything but total confidence.

'You're not going to turn me down, are you, sir?'

Alone in the waiting room, Alan tried hard not to feel too despondent. Commissioned officers and young gentlemen from public schools were finding it difficult enough to convince the interviewing officer of their suitability for training as pilots, so what chance did a blacksmith have?

He thought he heard the scrape of a chair in the interview room and he came to his feet, straightening his necktie and inspecting his hands yet again; he had spent most of the previous evening endeavouring to scrub away the dirt and grease ingrained by years of work in the smithy.

Charles came out of the interview room. He looked very serious. Then he saw Alan and his face broke into a delighted smile.

'He's giving me a shot at taking my ticket. Whatever that means.'

'Your pilot's certificate,' Alan explained, pleased at Charles's success. 'Congratulations!'

'Thanks! I'm to report on the ninth. Beechwood Reserve Squadron. I can't wait to tell them in the Mess. Oh – good luck!'

Alan thanked him, watched him go, then rapped on the door of the interview room.

'Come in!'

The Major was glancing at a letter. Alan recognized it as the letter of recommendation from Colonel Starke.

'Farmer, isn't it? Sit down, Farmer. How old are you?'

'Eighteen, sir.'

'You can count, I hope?' the Major enquired with a supercilious smile. 'Get a lot of chaps in here who can't.'

Alan assured him that he was eighteen last January and the Major looked at the letter.

'This Colonel Starke says you're just the chap we're looking for. Are you?'

'I hope so, sir.'

'The Colonel is a relative, is he?'

'No, sir.'

'I see. Friend of the family, eh? Says you're the best shot he's ever seen.'

'I was lucky that day, sir. They were running to my left.'

'They?'

'Rabbits, sir. When they're going to my right – I have been known to miss one.'

The Major smiled faintly and Alan allowed himself a smile in return.

'Can you ride a horse, Farmer?'

Alan said that he could. Then, knowing that the question

must be put to him sooner or later, he decided to get it over and done with.

'I can shoe one as well, sir.'

The Major sat upright in his chair.

'Shoe one?'

'I'm a blacksmith, sir.'

The Major frowned and looked at the Colonel's letter with the irritated air of a man who has been grossly deceived.

'I see to the Colonel's motor car,' Alan volunteered, a heaviness in his heart now. He added that the motor car was a Daimler but that didn't seem to help very much. The Major leaned back in his chair, said the Flying Corps was looking for blacksmiths and that Alan should apply to his nearest recruiting centre. 'I'd hoped for the chance to train as a pilot, sir.'

'I can't help you there, I'm afraid,' the Major said, rather impatiently. 'You need a commission.'

'But you do have some non-commissioned pilots, don't you, sir?'

'Yes, we do.' The Major's tone was coldly antagonistic. 'Chaps who have earned their chance to train as pilots. Starting as mechanics, become observers and put in their flying hours over enemy lines. You want to do it all in one gulp. You can't!'

Alan, shattered inside, made what he felt to be one last despairing effort.

'I believe you are taking some civilians now, sir.'

'Some. Yes. If a chap comes to us straight from school – from study – and playing the right sort of games.'

The Major looked at some papers on his desk and Alan wondered if he should leave of his own accord or wait to be dismissed. The Major sighed rather wearily.

'You're disappointed, I know. Been reading the magazines. *Flight* and *The Aero*. Pictures of the smiling aviators. If they can do it, so can you, eh?'

'If I had the chance, sir – I know I could take my ticket.'

'So you think I'm being unfair, eh?'

Alan looked at him steadfastly before he replied.

'Yes, sir. I suppose I do.'

'Look, Farmer. If you were a commissioned officer you'd have a head start. Shall I tell you why?'

'I think I know, sir,' Alan said politely. 'An officer is trained in military observation. So he'll know what to look for from the air. And the Royal Flying Corps is still very young, sir. So a commissioned officer helps to promote esprit de corps.'

The Major was mildly surprised.

'Know all the answers, do you, Farmer?'

'I've been reading books on flying since I was thirteen years old, sir.'

'Books won't help you to fly an aeroplane. For that, your brains need to be in your hands.'

'That's what my grandfather used to say, sir. About being a good blacksmith.'

The Major considered for a moment.

'You see to motor cars, eh? Ever seen a Gnome aero engine?'

'No, sir. But I've worked on a 35 hp Green.'

The Major blinked as Alan took the photograph from his wallet and placed it on the desk.

'Three years ago, sir. That's my father. That's Mr Starke – the owner of The Flyer. We rebuilt her. Well – I handed up the tools.'

The Major looked interested, smiled his approval, and Alan felt his hopes rising.

'Well, no doubt about you, is there, Farmer? An engine fitter. Two shillings a day and all found. How does that sound to you?'

'I'd be more value to the Flying Corps as a pilot, sir.'

'And no reason why you shouldn't become one,' the Major explained, trying to keep the irritation out of his voice. 'Start as a mechanic. You'll do some flying. You're a fair shot. You could go on to do some observing. Then worry us to send you home to train as a pilot.'

Alan looked fixedly down at the desk. The Major blew forcibly.

'I know. The war might end next week and you won't get your chance. Well, there is another way. Learn to fly at your own expense. Get your Aero Club Certificate and come back and see me again.'

'Seventy-five pounds,' Alan said quietly. 'It would take me years to save that amount, sir. And as I've already learned to fly – well – it's a lot of money for just a piece of paper.'

The Major stared at him.

'Already learned to fly?'

'When I was fifteen, sir. Mr Starke lent me a copy of Mr Graham-White's *How an Airman Learns to Fly* and I used to sit—'

'Mr Starke?'

Alan indicated the photograph of The Flyer on the desk.

'The owner of that machine, sir. We kept her in the barn and I'd go down there every evening to practise working the controls. Then Mr Starke used to let me taxi her round the field—'

The Major interrupted sharply.

'You mean to say you've been flying this machine?'

Alan looked at him steadily for a moment. The opportunity was Heaven-sent and he was unable to resist it.

'Yes, sir.'

The Major looked extremely irritated.

'Why the devil didn't you say so before? We could have waived all these damned silly questions.' And he was already scribbling on the pad in front of him. 'OC Beechwood Reserve Squadron on the ninth.'

Molly failed to understand why Alan was not being given a uniform. Harry explained that Alan was taking a test and would be home again in a few days.

'If he passes the test, if he gets his pilot's ticket, that is – then they'll give him a uniform and he'll start his training proper.'

He was having difficulty in putting a letter into an envelope and Molly did it for him.

'To the manager of Claybourne's factory in Caxton,' Harry explained. 'They're going over to munitions and he's offered me a job as watchdog to a lot of women.'

'Machine work,' Tom said disgustedly, as he came in from the yard. 'And women doing it. There's a recipe for poor quality if you like. I spoke to the missus, Harry. And you can move in when you like.'

Harry caught Molly's bewildered look and gave a little uncomfortable smile.

'I shall be looking for lodgings in Caxton,' he said. 'But until then – well – I can't very well stay on here, can I? Not with Alan out of the house.'

'Of course you can't,' Tom said in a stern voice. 'It wouldn't be proper.'

After the men had gone out, Molly put the clean shirts into Alan's suitcase, snapped the catches shut, wiped the dust from the lid with her sleeve, and looked around the kitchen.

Suddenly, she felt very alone.

'Beechwood is our newest Reserve Squadron,' the Adjutant explained to the six new arrivals. 'So you'll have to bear with the rather primitive accommodation and the lack of some of the more usual amenities, I'm afraid. You're here to have a shot at taking your ticket. Your pilot's certificate. As you may know, we're desperately short of machines. So we can't waste time with chaps who are not up to taking their tickets in – well – what may seem to some of you to be an alarmingly short time. However, there are chaps who can do it. Those are the chaps we want.'

Alan and Charles exchanged confident smiles.

'Those chaps will go on to fly the Avro and the BE2,' the Adjutant went on. 'If and when they are available. When they've gone solo on those machines, can do satisfactory flights by compass, have passed their tests in lamp signalling, engine fitting and rigging – then they'll be able to put up their wings.' And he paused to allow the keen young faces to bask in this thrilling vision. 'They will then be posted to a Squadron for further training and to put in the required number of hours before being sent to a Squadron in France.'

He paused again and Alan imagined he could hear the

rumble of gunfire and the sound of the engines as the Squadron took off, heading east for the enemy lines.

'For civilians, of course, it's rather different. They will need to do their initial army training first. Their feet firmly on the ground. And in a strong pair of boots.'

Alan and the one other civilian exchanged rueful smiles. Charles asked if their instructor had been appointed.

'Yes, indeed,' the Adjutant replied. 'You'll all be with Captain Triggers. He's a very experienced flier. Flew one of the first machines on the Western Front.'

They all looked suitably impressed and the Adjutant wished them luck and turned to leave the hut. Then a thought occurred to him.

'Ah, yes. Farmer? You've already done some flying, of course.'

Alan's fingers froze on the catches of his suitcase. He felt all eyes upon him as he nodded and said yes, he had done.

'You're a dark horse, I must say,' Charles said when the Adjutant had gone. 'You told me you hadn't done any flying.'

'I haven't,' Alan said quietly, glancing around to make sure the others were not listening. They were all too busy unpacking. 'You see – it was my only chance.'

Charles stared at him in admiration.

'Lord! That took some pluck.'

'Not really. I said it without even thinking.'

'Oh. I see.'

They went on unpacking, carefully, like men walking on thin ice. Charles seemed far more concerned than Alan.

'I'm rather worried about you,' Charles said at last. 'Look. It's no use sticking your head in a sack and hoping for the best. It won't work tomorrow, now will it? I mean supposing they ask you to show them what you can do?' And he stared down at his bed as if the thought was too hair-raising to voice. Then he came to a decision. 'Talk to the Adjutant. Right now. Make a clean breast.'

Alan looked at him and went on unpacking.

'It's different for you,' he said. 'But for me – well – it would hardly be worth my unpacking this suitcase.'

Charles nodded. He thought he understood. The chap was a blacksmith. No education. Nothing to recommend him apart from the lie he had told.

'Lord, you've brought enough shirts, haven't you?'

'My mother,' Alan smiled. 'She wants me to look my best because – well, I'll be mixing with chaps like you.'

Their eyes held for a moment. They went on unpacking.

'Here, I've got it!' Charles said at last. 'Our instructor! Captain Triggers! Flying chaps are different. The ones who actually fly, I mean. I've heard they don't care two hoots for rules and regulations. Some of them even like flaunting them, they say. If he's decent – and he's bound to be – he'll understand that you lied because you were desperately keen.'

At that moment, the hut door burst open and Captain Triggers came in. He was in a state of barely contained fury and every man stopped what he was doing and came instinctively to attention.

'If your engine cuts on take-off – never turn back. Never! Do you understand? Get that into your heads now. This minute! This second! I wasn't here to welcome you because I was at the hospital. Looking at an idiot who thought he *could* turn back – in spite of having my warning burned into his skull.' He looked at each of the men in turn as if unable to decide which of them to tear apart first. 'Let me welcome you with this. You're not here to learn to fly. Understand? You're here to save your skins. Think of it that way – and you may live to learn to fly.'

And he turned and walked out, slamming the door behind him.

'Lord!' Charles exclaimed and turned to look sympathetically at Alan.

chapter nine

'She looks like a bathtub with wings,' Charles remarked as he and Alan made their way to the bench outside the aeroplane shed and sat there watching the Farman 'Longhorn' taking off, flying a few feet above the ground and landing again.

'The pupil's flying "straights",' Alan explained. 'When you can fly "straights" to the instructor's satisfaction then you go on to fly in a circular motion around the field and land in the same direction in which you took off. That's called a circuit.'

'A little mine of information, aren't you?' Charles said, testily. Then he forced a grin. 'Sorry! But I've never been so nervous in all my life. I see why they give us these helmets now. You strap them on tight and they stop your teeth from chattering.'

'I'm nervous, too,' Alan said quietly.

'So you damned well ought to be. What if Captain Triggers asks you to take her up on your own?'

'I shouldn't think he will. He'll probably come with me. Ask me to show him what I can do.'

Charles gave a little shudder.

'Rather you than me. I mean the way he put the wind up us all last night. The very thought of you being alone up there in the sky with him when he finds out you've been lying . . .' He stopped, staring towards the hut from which a man had just emerged. 'Lord, talk of the devil.'

With fixed glazed smiles and wildly beating hearts they both stood up in readiness to greet their instructor. Captain Triggers appeared to be in the best of spirits as he walked briskly towards them, waving cheerily to the mechanics who were wheeling an Avro 504 on to the field. The mechanics waved back uncertainly and their wary smiles told the two young men that Captain Triggers was a man whose moods underwent swift and violent change.

'Good morning, gentlemen,' he beamed sunnily. 'Which of you is Mr Gay Lion?'

Charles winced slightly at the mispronunciation of his name and cleared his throat.

'I'm Gaylion, sir.'

'The Longhorn for you.' And he turned to Alan. 'You're Mr Farmer then. You've done some flying, I hear. You haven't flown an Avro though, I take it?'

'No, sir, I haven't.'

'You'll like the Avro. Sit in the front cockpit and tickle the controls while I start Mr Gay Lion wondering why he wants to leave the cavalry. I'll join you in twenty minutes. Right, Gay Lion! Off we go!'

'It's pronounced "Gaylion", sir,' Charles said politely as he hurried after Triggers. And he cast an anxious glance at Alan who was already on his way to the Avro. 'Will Mr Farmer be taking the Avro up on his own, sir?'

'What's that to do with you?' Triggers snapped. 'Well, come on, man. Put your foot on the tyre and climb up. No stirrups on these, you know, or batmen to give you a leg-up. No, don't put your foot there, you idiot. It'll go right through. And whatever you do, for God's sake don't stand up. You're a bit of a Goliath and you'll stall her.'

'She looks rather like a toboggan at the front,' Charles remarked, wondering what the devil his heart was doing beating away in his stomach.

'That's to save young necks like yours. Chaps who think they can land in a vertical position.' He waved impatiently to the mechanic who was sauntering up. 'Not keeping you waiting, am I?' And he pointed to behind Charles's head. 'The engine's behind you, so your bottom will be nice and warm, at least.'

'A pusher,' Charles said, airing the knowledge he had picked up from Alan. 'A seventy-horse-power Renault.'

Triggers smiled wisely at the determinedly brave but ghastly white young face.

'This rather delicate coffin in which we are sitting is called the nacelle,' Triggers explained. 'It's just been freshly doped. So if you think you're going to be sick, Gay Lion – kindly lean well out.'

Under the bored gaze of a mechanic who sat chewing a blade of grass, Alan assumed a casual air, climbed into the cockpit of the Avro and proceeded to 'test the controls'. He knew the theory of their functions well enough; but putting the theory into practice for the very first time whilst the Avro was in flight was quite another matter. He practised pushing and pulling the control lever and see-sawing his feet on the pedal-bar whilst carefully observing the corresponding movements of the ailerons, elevator and rudder, although he knew it was a hopeless task to try and assess what effect the degree of movement would have on the machine whilst in flight.

He watched the Longhorn performing 'straights' and envied Charles Gaylion with nothing more expected of him than to prove that he could 'take his ticket' within the allotted time. Alan had confidence enough in his ability to do just that. But to fly an aeroplane when he had never even been up in one before, and to fly it well enough to convince Captain Triggers that he had not lied to the interviewing officer ... However, that was exactly what he had to do, and his chance to train as a pilot in the Royal Flying Corps depended on it.

He watched the Longhorn take off and rise above the trees at the far end of the field and thought of The Flyer on that June afternoon almost three years ago. He remembered the explosion and his father's body wreathed in flames.

'You starting her up, sir?' the mechanic enquired.

'Er – no, not yet. I'm waiting for Captain Triggers.'

'Wind's freshening!' Triggers exclaimed, waving the mechanic to 'suck in'. 'Better go while we can, Mr Farmer. A left-hand turn. A right-hand turn. And bring her down. That's all I want you to do. Now. Very important. Hand signals, so we both know what we're doing.' And he leaned forward and thumped Alan's right shoulder. 'I shall bang you like that and shout "you've got her". If for any reason you wish to hand her back to me, you shout "you've got her" and take your hands and feet off the controls. And hold your hands up for me to *see*. We're not magical minds in a music hall. Switch on!'

'Switch on!' the mechanic called and swung the propeller.

The engine roared into life and a few minutes later Alan soared into the air for the very first time in his life. Glancing back at the field he saw Charles's broad encouraging wave. This was it! He had been thrown in at the deep end and now he had to swim as boldly as he could. Or drown!

'You've got her!'

As Triggers's hand thumped his shoulder Alan grabbed the control lever and slid his feet on to the pedal-bar. He lurched forward as the nose dropped, yanked at the lever and saw the horizon disappear. She was climbing! He took a deep breath, steadied himself, moved the lever forward until he saw the horizon appear again, glanced at the wingtips, saw the port wingtip had dropped and eased the lever to starboard to bring it up. He checked the nose once again, decided she was flying straight and level, and continued flying steadily on for a time, his feet resting lightly on the pedal-bar, his fingers curled gently about the control-lever as if their strength might crush it. The machine was flying itself; he was simply a watchful sentinel, ready to correct any untoward movements, and with a surge of confidence he see-sawed the pedal-bar in order to feel the yawing effect of the rudder before attempting to make a left-hand turn. The turns would be more difficult, he knew that. And as for bringing her down ... well! He'd think about that when the time came.

Tentatively, he pushed left rudder and eased the control lever over, his eyes fixed on the horizon. She was turning! And a good turn, he thought. He wasn't losing or gaining height. Now – how far to turn, that was the question? Ninety degrees, it should be. He hadn't considered that. Damn! He should have found a landmark to turn on to. Never mind! No use worrying over that now. He wasn't doing too badly. In fact, he was doing rather well, he thought, and he eased the stick back to the central position and released the pressure on the pedal-bar, so that he was flying straight and level once again.

He resisted an almost overwhelming urge to look around at Captain Triggers to try and guess what the man was thinking of his performance. His instinct told him that Triggers must be thinking he was doing rather well and without further ado he pushed right rudder and went into the right-hand turn.

'Lord!' Charles cried, jumping up from the bench as the Avro side-slipped.

'Bit o' slip, that's all, sir,' the mechanic said with a practised air of boredom. He had been in the Corps all of two months and 'death and destruction' was part of his daily routine. He yawned at the waggling wings as the Avro came out of the turn. 'They'll stand a lot, them Avros.'

'He's doing rather well, isn't he?' Charles enquired, anxious for the opinion of an expert.

'He's a blacksmith, I hear.'

'That's right.'

The mechanic sniffed.

'Ordinary blokes don't stand a chance of training for pilots,' he grumbled. 'That's what they told *me*.'

'It's different for Alan. He's already a flier.'

'We'll know that when he's made his landing, sir,' the mechanic said with a knowledgeable smirk. 'That's what sorts the fliers from the duds. Three weeks I've been here – and nine crashes on landings.'

'Alan won't crash,' Charles said, anxiously willing Alan to hand the Avro back to Triggers when it was time to put her down.

'Take her down!' Triggers bawled, thumping Alan on the shoulder.

'Right, sir!' Alan called back confidently. He looked to one side, then the other. Where the hell had the airfield gone? It was behind him, of course. It had to be! But he dare not look around in case Triggers saw the panic in his face. He had made a left-hand turn and then a right-hand turn, so the airfield must be somewhere to starboard and a few miles behind. He looked. No sign of it. Wasn't on the port side, either.

'Down there!' Triggers shouted. And again when Alan gaped. 'Down there!'

Alan looked over the side. The airfield was directly beneath. Striving to keep calm, he made a shaky left-hand turn, flew on for several minutes, and made another. The airfield was directly ahead now. He eased the stick forward and cut the engine.

'Lord!' Charles exclaimed, as he watched the yawing Avro making its approach. 'It's coming in rather steeply, isn't it?'

The mechanic's eyes were alight with the exciting prospect of yet another crash.

'We'll have the farmer complaining again. We've had four down in that wheatfield.'

Alan's eyes were fixed intently on the airfield. He eased the stick to bring the nose up slightly, then a little push to star-board as the port wing dropped. Yes, he was going to make the field just nicely. More luck than judgement though, he knew that. He tensed himself for the landing and remembered Conway Starke's advice to his father: 'Don't put her down until you can see the separate blades of grass.'

'Is he blind or something?' the mechanic muttered. 'Why doesn't he switch the bloody engine on?'

'Switch the engine on!' Charles cried in desperation.

Alan saw the hedge looming up and realized with horror that he wasn't going to make the field after all. If he pulled the stick back he'd stall her. What was he to do?

'I've got her!' Triggers bawled, switching on the engine.

Charles felt sick with relief as the Avro skimmed the hedge and touched down just inside the field.

'You're a damned liar!' Triggers shouted. He was white with fury as he tugged off his flying helmet. 'And you'd have killed us both sooner than admit it. Why the hell didn't you hand her back to me?'

Alan just sat there in the cockpit. He wanted to say that he thought he could make the field, that it was simply a case of misjudgement, but he could not find the words.

'Lying is one thing, for God's sake. Stubborn stupidity is another.' Raging now, he shoved his face into Alan's. 'Do you know what my life is worth in this game, Farmer? Three ha'pence at most. But clever souls like you would have me give it away.'

And he stormed off in the direction of the sheds. Alan, shattered and shame-faced, climbed out of the cockpit. The mechanic smiled consolingly.

'One thing. You won't have his vicious tongue to put up with no more.'

But the mechanic was wrong. An hour later, when Alan had almost finished packing his suitcase, Triggers strode into the hut.

'Home to mother, eh?' Triggers said, icily vindictive. 'They tell me you're a blacksmith.'

'Yes, sir.'

'No wonder you're so heavy-handed.'

Alan lowered his eyes under the force of the man's gaze.

'Pleased with yourself, are you? I suppose you think you could have landed her, too, if I hadn't interfered?'

'No, sir,' Alan said, barely audible. 'I would have crashed her.'

'Do you really think I left her to you up there?' And he slammed down the lid of the suitcase, forcing Alan to meet his gaze. 'Thought you were flying her yourself, did you, with no help at all from me? D'you think I didn't know in the first minute that you'd never flown a machine before?'

This was the final humiliation for Alan. And Triggers was there to enjoy every ounce of it.

'Do you know what would have happened if I *had* left her to you up there?'

'Yes, sir.'

'Oh, you know, eh?' Triggers said, with biting sarcasm. 'You've never been up in a machine before today but you know all the hazards?'

'I've read about them, sir,' Alan said, lamely.

'Reading is one thing, experience is another,' Triggers snapped. 'You've read about spinning, no doubt?'

Yes, Alan had read about spinning. It was to be avoided at all costs. Spinning meant certain death; and no one knew the cause of it.

'I'll tell you the cause of it,' Triggers hissed. 'Idiots like you! Who think flying is easy and are willing to chance their lives and the lives of chaps like me in order to prove it. But all soldiers are brave until they feel the point of a bayonet at their throats.' There was a vengeful gleam in his eyes now. He glanced at Alan's suitcase. 'Catching the next train, are you?'

'No, sir. I've got a motor cycle.'

'Good! Then we've time for a fond farewell.'

Alan thought the Avro would never stop climbing. His feet and hands were numb with cold and he wanted more than anything to slide his body down inside the cockpit to shield his face from the bitter wind that lashed his frozen cheeks. But he was in the front cockpit under Triggers's fierce gaze and so was determined to remain 'upright and fearless' in order to show the man that he was ready to face whatever was in store for him. Triggers had made his intention quite clear, of course. The 'fond farewell' was to be a harsh lesson that Alan would never forget; a reprimand for lying at the interview and for foolishly spurning the hazards that might have spelled death for Alan and his instructor. Yet Alan bore no ill-feeling towards the man. In fact, he was grateful to Triggers, despite the discomfort of the bitingly cold air and the growing alarm he was striving desperately to control. Instead of slinking home with his tail between his legs he could at least leave Beechwood with his head held high, having taken his punishment like a man.

As they went on climbing, Alan looked down at the earth far below and recalled that the Avro 504 had set a British altitude record of fourteen thousand feet in February 1914 and he felt a strong surge of pride in the fact that he was actually flying in a machine that had performed that great feat. Then he thought of his mother's face when he arrived home that evening to tell her that he had failed to be accepted for training as a pilot. Oh, she'd make a show of being disappointed at his failure but she'd be secretly relieved, of course. And a heavy despair filled his heart. The new life he had dreamed of ever since he was a schoolboy and which had begun only yesterday was already at an end. The great adventure was over before it had begun. Ferocity welled up in him at the unfairness of the circumstances which had provoked him into lying at the interview. He wanted to turn round and blaze defiance at the man in the cockpit behind him; to tell him that no matter what hazards he was put through he would remain unflinching. He'd show them the mettle of the young man they were turning down; what a great mistake they were making. But he knew in his heart that he was simply feeling sorry for himself. He had no one to blame but himself for what had happened. And the man sitting behind him was putting him through this chastening experience not out of petty vengeance or vindictiveness but to show Alan that human life was more important than selfish ambition. Alan sensed a deep compassion in the man that commanded his respect. Triggers's rages seemed to Alan not to be directed at the men about him but at their common enemy – death! He felt he could have wished for nothing better than to train as a pilot under such a man. And he cursed himself as the hot angry tears sprang to his eyes. He had not felt like this since the day of his father's funeral, when he'd been angry with fate for causing his mother so much pain and with himself for crying at the graveside when she had remained so brave and dignified.

The Avro levelled out and almost immediately canted over into a steeply banked turn. Taken unawares, Alan clutched the rim of the cockpit and glanced back at Triggers, who smiled thinly, gave a little menacing wave, and proceeded to roll the Avro into an even steeper turn on the opposite bank. Alan hung grimly on, his stomach caught in steel jaws, the corners of his mouth pulled down by invisible strings. And suddenly they were climbing again. Then the engine stopped and the Avro hung in the air. God, what had gone wrong? Triggers gave a gesture of despair in reply to Alan's enquiring glance, then, as if someone had planted a giant heel on it, the Avro's tail slammed down. Alan screamed an involuntary protest as he fell backwards into the hole in the heavens, the Avro lurching and whistling about him, a drunken machine with no sense of purpose or direction. A long crazy sigh was abruptly cut off by the clack-clacking of the propeller blades and the ominous whirring of a thousand birdwings as the flashing sky became revolving earth. Alan sucked air into his quivering lungs and he realized the Avro was in the throes of certain death. She was spinning! The hazard so feared by beginners and experienced fliers alike. Once in a spin there was absolutely no escape. They would now go on spinning until they hit the ground. He was going to die. The ground was coming closer and closer. God, dear God, he prayed, forgive me for lying at the interview, forgive me ... I didn't intend to ... take care of my mother ... she's been hurt so much already ...

And the earth stopped turning as Alan's body threatened to push itself through the bottom of the fuselage, the sky appeared between the wings and the engine was on. Alan leaned out of the cockpit to survey the precious countryside that he would soon be walking once again, then heaved his breakfast over it.

Charles was napping blissfully when Triggers stamped into the hut.

'Not keeping you waiting, am I?' Triggers snapped.

Charles leapt to his feet, goggling at Alan who dragged his leaden feet over to his bed and stood there, white and shaken.

'You'd better sit down before you fall down,' Triggers said, contemptuously. Alan remained doggedly on his feet. Triggers turned to Charles. 'Is that your motor car out there?'

'Yes, sir.'

'Quite a beauty.'

Charles was pleased.

'I pity her at the mercy of *your* loving hands,' Triggers added. 'Still. Sweat a bit and you might manage to take your ticket.'

'Thank you, sir,' Charles said, brightening.

'Don't thank me. You'll earn it, believe me.' He jerked his head at the open door and Charles hurried out. Triggers pursed his lips and glared balefully at Alan. 'About the flying you're supposed to have done. I shall tell the Adjutant you've picked up a lot of bad habits. You'll start from scratch the same as the others.'

Alan could hardly believe his ears.

'Be out there in half an hour,' Triggers ordered sharply. And stamped out.

*

Molly was making the bread when Alan arrived and her hands were covered in flour.

'It's only for the weekend,' Alan explained breathlessly, glad to see her, but full of his new life. 'I'm flying again on Monday morning. Captain Triggers says I've an even chance of taking my ticket.'

'Well, fancy that. Lorna was here. If you'd been just two minutes earlier ...' She broke off, staring at the bunch of flowers he held out to her. 'Oh. My hands! All flour!'

'Charles was buying some. I was in the shop with him and so – well – I thought you'd like some.'

She was still staring at them when Harry came in from the smithy.

'They haven't managed to stop him rushing about,' she said. 'He's gone running after Lorna. He's going back on Monday.'

'Yes, he said.' Harry had something on his mind and was wondering how to put it. 'Tom and I have been talking. But I said we ought to wait and see whether Alan was joining the Flying Corps or not. It looks as if he is, so – well – you'll be short of a man here.' He waited for some comment but she was still staring at the flowers. 'I could do odd jobs. Fetch and carry. But as I said to Tom, it's up to you. You're the boss here now.'

Molly looked at him in surprise.

'What about the job they offered you at Claybourne's?'

'Watchdog over a lot of women.' Harry grinned self-consciously. 'They'll soon find someone else for that, I should think.'

Their eyes held for a brief moment. Then Molly looked back at the flowers; still a wonder to her.

'It would only be for the time being, of course,' Harry said. 'Until you find another man, that is.'

'You'd live at Tom's place?'

'He won't have me go anywhere else.'

'Fancy that. I mean – you back here working, after all these years.' And she gave a little laugh. 'We'll have to talk about a wage for you then.'

Lorna had almost reached the barn when Alan caught her up.

'I remember you sitting in there on the summer evenings,' she said. 'Working The Flyer's controls. So I'm pleased you've got what you want.'

'You won't miss me then?' Alan said, looking up at the sky as if not caring what her answer would be.

'I might,' Lorna said, smiling prettily. 'I can't wait to see you in the uniform. So far I've only seen pictures of it in the magazines.'

'It won't look right. Not for a bit.'

'Not right? How d'you mean – not right?'

He smiled, and with a newfound boldness, took her hand in his.

'Just here,' he said, touching his left breast. 'That's where they put the wings.'

chapter ten

The early morning April air was damp and cold and Alan was sure he could already smell the frying bacon and eggs in the pupils' Mess as he cut the engine, went into a spiral turn to lose height, and floated like thistledown on to the field.

The other bed in his room was occupied by Sergeant Mac-Iver, a tough Scot who had flown as an observer in France and had arrived the day before to commence his training as a pilot.

'Rise and shine!' Alan called cheerily, clanking the metal mug against the plate. 'Or you'll miss your breakfast.'

'You'll be missing your head if you don't shut up,' MacIver threatened, peering belligerently from the igloo of bedclothes. He sat up, his hands pressed to the sides of his aching head. He had spent his first night back in Blighty celebrating at the Blue Anchor and looked at Alan as if he were an apparition. 'Flying before breakfast?'

'The only way to get my hours in,' Alan said brightly, taking off his flying coat. 'One Avro between ten of us. Half an hour this morning. So that makes six hours now.'

'Wait until you've done forty over enemy lines,' MacIver grumbled. He had been a mechanic before becoming an observer and so had earned his chance to train as a pilot. 'You schoolboy pilots have it too easy.'

'I left school when I was fourteen,' Alan smiled.

'Aye, I heard you were a special case,' MacIver said as he pulled on his breeches. 'And they tell me you're pretty good.'

'I'm the only one who hasn't crashed a bus yet,' Alan said modestly, carefully folding his scarf.

'They were saying about your father.'

Alan placed the scarf in its place in the locker and indicated

Triggers's do's and don't's written up on the inside of the locker door.

'Number One is the biggest killer. If your engine fails on take-off, never turn back to the field. Get your nose down to maintain flying speed and look for a suitable place to land.'

'That what your father did? Tried to turn back?'

'Yes. It was his first solo. The engine failed and he turned back to the field. She hit some trees and caught fire.'

MacIver was grimly thoughtful as he picked up his soap, razor and towel.

'A terrible thing, fire. You saw it happen, eh?'

'Yes, I did.'

'If I'd seen that happen to my father it would have put me off this flying lark for good, I know that.' It was almost a question and he waited for Alan's comment.

'He shouldn't have turned back,' Alan said, quite simply.

'You're the one who never makes a mistake, eh?' MacIver's tone was derisive. This cocky youngster. All confidence and neatness. Everything in his bed-space in its proper place. Just wait until he got to France. 'Abiding by the rules is all very well over here. But they won't keep you alive over there. More to flying an aeroplane than taking off, landing, and making right and left-hand turns.'

'Not here, there isn't,' Alan grinned. 'God help you if you break one of Captain Triggers's do's and don't's.'

'Bloody strange, isn't it? Triggers, I mean. Me flying with him as his observer. Now he'll be teaching me to fly.'

Alan was intent on his reflection in the mirror as he buttoned up his 'maternity jacket'. He was eyeing the left breast as MacIver's head appeared over his shoulder.

'See the wings already, can you?' MacIver said, with a little twisting smile. 'Let's hope they're the right sort. Not the ones that go with a harp.'

'You're a cheery sort, aren't you, MacIver?'

'*Sergeant* MacIver to you,' MacIver snapped. 'You haven't got your wings yet. You're still a second class AM. The lowest form of animal. And don't you forget it. As for making mistakes, you can learn from wee ones, you know. But the feller who never makes one at all ... he can end up making the biggest one of the lot.'

The pupils' Mess was noisy with anticipation of the day's flying when Charles Gaylion hurried in. Alan was sitting with MacIver and another young civilian entrant, a public schoolboy named Roger Pearson. Charles moved stealthily up to the table and stood behind Alan.

'Under the spreading chestnut tree ... the flying blacksmith lands.'

Alan stared in delighted surprise.

'Charles! What are you doing here?'

'All stations to St Omer. Via Folkestone and Calais.'

'Posted to France? You're not? You lucky dog!'

'But I didn't count on a dud engine. And a brand new bus, too.'

'Some say good old Royal Aircraft Factory,' MacIver commented, dourly. 'No wonder half our fellers never get to France. Our machines are the real enemy, not the Hun.' He scowled at Pearson's grinning face. 'And that's no joke, old son.'

Alan pulled Charles's flying coat aside to reveal the wings on the tunic breast. Charles smiled at Alan's good-natured envy.

'Don't worry, you'll get yours soon enough. They're so short of pilots they're giving them to dud fliers, too.'

'Alan's no dud,' Pearson said, defensively. 'He's the best flier in our lot.'

'The flying blacksmith. Steady and reliable, eh?'

Charles's tone was light-hearted, but MacIver sensed a bite in it and decided he wasn't too keen on Second-Lieutenant Charles Gaylion. And the bloody superior way he asked Alan to fetch some breakfast for him after enquiring if they would 'serve a fully fledged chap in the pupils' Mess' ...

'I took my ticket here at Beechwood, along with Alan. But he was held up. Had to do his initial army training.'

'So did I,' Pearson said with a groan. 'Sticking bayonets in sandbags and marching up and down. Beastly rotten waste of

131

time. I could have been in France by now. Shooting down Huns.'

Charles's face straightened.

'That's hardly our object, is it? Our role in this war is reconnaissance.'

'Not according to Captain Triggers,' Pearson said, stirring his coffee. 'He's showing us how to kill Huns before they kill us.'

MacIver winced. The bravado of these schoolboys embarrassed him.

'Captain Triggers is simply teaching you how to defend yourselves in the air,' he said.

'What's the difference?' Pearson retorted. 'Anyway, you shot down a Hun.' And he explained to Charles how Sergeant MacIver and Captain Triggers had made a lone raid on a German airfield. 'Got a Hun just as he was taking off.'

Charles eyed MacIver with cold disapproval.

'He couldn't have had much of a chance, I'd say.'

'It's not all you might think it is "over there",' MacIver said, meeting Charles's condemning gaze.

'Triggers is giving a lecture on air fighting this morning, as a matter of fact,' Pearson said, suggesting that Charles might attend as he was not flying to France until the following day.

'They're seeing to my engine this morning,' Charles said. 'But I'm taking no chances. I want to give her a thorough test before I go.'

'Tomorrow?' Alan said, arriving at the table with Charles's bacon and eggs. 'Then I shan't be here to see you off. I'm going home today.'

'Sunday tomorrow,' MacIver said. 'Is it worth going home for one night?'

'As long as he's home before milking time,' Pearson grinned.

'Ah, so it's still the farmer's daughter then?' Charles smiled across at Alan's reddening features. 'Here, you're not married or anything . . . ?'

'Of course not,' Alan said, tightly.

'Shouldn't waste any time, old son,' Pearson said. 'We'll be "over there" soon enough, you know.'

Anxious to change the subject, Alan asked Charles how many hours he had flown.

'Fourteen!'

'A feller needs fifty at least before being sent over enemy lines,' MacIver said, dourly.

'Not that pilots count,' Pearson gave a sly wink at the others. 'The observer's the important chap.'

'And so he is,' MacIver said, truculently. 'The pilot's just a chauffeur.'

'So why do *you* want to be a pilot?' Pearson enquired with studied innocence.

'Because my life will be in my own two hands, that's why. Not in the inky fingers of some schoolboy pilot with fourteen hours—' MacIver broke off, biting his lip. His reply was intended for Pearson but applied equally to Charles, of course.

'It's not the number of hours that counts,' Charles said, smiling blandly. 'It's making the best use of them. Do you know why so many of our chaps go west?' And he looked pointedly at Alan. 'Because they obey the rules.'

Alan glanced at MacIver who had said something to the same effect earlier that morning. Pearson didn't understand, so Charles explained.

'It's quite simple. *You* may obey the rules – but your poor old machine won't. Aeroplanes are like horses. They get restless now and again. Suddenly do something you don't expect them to do.'

'Like stalling and going into a spin, you mean?' Pearson said, expressing the dread they all felt at the very mention of these hazards. 'Then all one can do is to pray.'

'I'd rather face an enemy than have him catch me unawares,' Charles said, his eyes meeting Alan's interested gaze. 'Wouldn't you?' Alan smiled his appreciation as Charles went on. 'A chap at Upavon showed me how. Been flying for five years and survived eleven crashes. A couple of bad ones, too. Come up to five thousand and stay on my tail, he said. You get the wind-up. But you learn. And fast.' He paused, looking

133

at their faces; Pearson's awed and impressed, Alan's keenly thoughtful, MacIver's grimly wary. 'What's wrong? I'm still alive, aren't I? And I've a good chance of staying that way. And believe me – half the things they tell us an aeroplane won't stand up to, is absolute rot.'

'What about the other half?' MacIver enquired, cunningly.

'That's just it. That's why you have to be on the tail of a chap who knows what he's doing.'

'You were jolly lucky to find such a chap,' Pearson said.

'I'm prepared to pass the benefit on to anyone who's interested,' Charles offered.

'What a pity,' Pearson said, trying his best to look disappointed. 'I'm not down for flying today.'

'What about you, Alan?'

Charles's tone was rather too offhand and MacIver gave Alan a fixed warning look.

'We've got Triggers's lecture at ten o'clock . . .' Alan began.

'Defending ourselves in the air,' Charles said, with a superior smile. 'There's only one way to do that. Beat our biggest enemy. Our rotten old machines.' And he gave a little triumphant smile at MacIver. 'Isn't that right, sergeant?'

MacIver was silent. Alan made his decision.

'After Triggers's lecture, if no one crashes the Avro and the wind doesn't get up, I shall be on a thirty-minute course by compass—'

'If Triggers finds out, he'll have your ears,' MacIver interrupted, sharply.

'Alan will be well out of range of his hawk-eyes, won't he?' Charles said, and seeing Alan's hesitation, added: 'As I say, it takes a bit of nerve.'

That was all Alan needed.

'Thanks for the offer, Charles.'

'My pleasure,' Charles smiled. 'A farewell gift, shall we say?'

When Captain Triggers had finished demonstrating an observer's difficulties in defending a BE2 armed only with a Winchester repeating rifle, he took the .45 Webley revolver from Sergeant MacIver and held it up for the assembled trainees to see.

'The forty-five Webley-Scott. The most I ever did with it was to slice one of my own bracing wires. However, the forty-five is the pilot's means of self-defence, and it does have its uses.'

And he looked at MacIver in a way that suggested to Alan that the two men shared some grim secret. Charles had come into the shed soon after the lecture had begun and was standing just behind MacIver. He had been listening in cold disapproval, unnoticed by Triggers, until this moment.

'Ah, Gay Lion! I was told you were here. So you're off to France tomorrow? Fourteen hours, eh? I hope you've made the best possible use of them?'

'I think I have, sir,' Charles said, quietly confident.

Triggers nodded, wished him luck, and said that he would buy him a farewell drink in the Blue Anchor that evening. Then he nodded towards Alan, seated in the rear cockpit of the BE2. 'And I shouldn't trouble to say farewell to Farmer here. He'll soon be hot on your tail.'

Charles and Alan exchanged swift glances at the irony of this remark, and for a moment Alan felt sure that Triggers suspected the arrangement they had made in the mess that morning.

'No, Triggers doesn't know, how could he?' MacIver said as he lay on his bed watching Alan putting on his flying gear. 'And no reason why he should find out, o' course. But I still think you're a fool accepting that Gaylion feller's challenge.'

'Challenge?' Alan grinned. 'Hardly that. He's doing it for my benefit, isn't he?'

MacIver looked sourly up at the flaking paint on the ceiling. 'Why isn't he off to France *now* instead of waiting till tomorrow?' he mused. 'He's got his engine fixed, hasn't he?'

'What's on your mind?' Alan snapped.

'Same as what's on yours. We both know, don't we? Your friend Charles has got cold feet.' His expression hardened under Alan's threatening look. 'What do you make of him

135

then? All that fuss over one Hun. You'd think I'd put a bullet through his mother.'

'He's entitled to his own opinion.'

'And what's that? They're the enemy, aren't they?'

Alan was determined not to get into an argument. He felt a strong sense of loyalty to Charles that he could never have explained to MacIver. So whether he found himself agreeing with MacIver's view or not was entirely beside the point.

'It affects fellers different ways,' MacIver went on. 'I remember the day before I went "over there". I'd never had a fight before in my life. That day – two drinks and I put a feller in hospital. Like a madman, I was. So you see, that pal of yours – you're getting the rough end of it. He may not know it – but he's spoiling for a fight.'

'Spoiling for a fight? Just now you accused him of having cold feet. Doesn't make much sense to me.'

'Neither do you!' MacIver said with sudden and surprising vehemence. He sat up on the bed. 'No crashes! No mistakes! And now suddenly you go behaving like an irresponsible—' He broke off with a sharp sigh and lay back on the bed again. 'Ah, go on. Get on with it. Go'n kill yourself like your father.'

Alan looked at him for a moment, then picked up the map and the clipboard from his bed.

'You're going ahead with it, then?' MacIver asked.

'I have to now,' Alan said, quietly. 'Or he'll think *I've* got cold feet.'

'Better cold feet than being roasted alive.'

Alan smiled. He liked MacIver.

'Thanks, anyway,' he said as he went out.

Charles's BE2 roared overhead as Alan asked permission to take off in the Avro. Triggers did not reply. His eyes were fixed on the BE2 as it banked steeply, the undercart just clearing the trees behind the sheds.

'Gay Lion! Fourteen hours in his book and already a three ring circus.' He looked witheringly after the climbing BE2 and when he turned to Alan his tone was heavy with implication. 'Thirty-minute flight by compass, Farmer.'

Enough said! Alan was rather relieved as he climbed into the Avro. There was no question of taking up Charles's 'challenge' now. Triggers was suspicious and if he found out that Alan had deliberately broken the rules it could well mean the end of Alan's career as a pilot. Charles would understand, of course, Alan was certain of that.

MacIver, all set for his first lesson in the Farman, stood alongside Triggers to watch the Avro taking off.

'There's your example, Sergeant MacIver. Farmer's a splendid pilot. Calm and methodical. Sticks to the rules like a leech. Now. You've had my list of do's and don'ts?'

'Yes, sir.'

'Number One?'

'If your engine fails on take-off, never turn back. Get your nose down to maintain flying speed and look for a suitable place to land.'

'Number Two?'

'Before a crash landing – always switch off to avoid the risk of fire.'

These words seemed to have a special meaning for them both and they were silent as they walked towards the Farman.

Just south of Shoreham, Alan turned the Avro on to the second leg of the triangular route he was required to fly and waited for the compass needle to settle down. The course was 030 degrees but the flickering needle showed 045. Alan ignored it. Triggers had warned them that the compass in an aeroplane was notoriously erratic and the only safe method of navigation in the air was by constant reference to the map, checking landmarks such as towns, rivers, railway junctions and unusual topographical features. This was also good practice for their role as 'the eyes of the army' when they were eventually posted to the Western Front.

The Western Front! The very sound of those words sent a shiver of excitement through Alan. He couldn't wait to be 'over there'; flying over enemy lines, ranging for the British artillery and putting in his observation reports, which together with the reports from his fellow fliers would provide the vital information needed for victory. And thrilling with pride at the importance of the role he was soon to be playing, he imagined enemy Archie shells bursting around his brave machine whilst the observer looked through his binoculars to gain the information that would 'turn the tide'. And then – the supreme excitement! His first glimpse of a Hun machine. It was streaking towards him on the starboard side.

It was a BE2, of course, and as it climbed above him, the pilot waved, and Alan realized it was Charles, keeping his 'appointment'. The BE2 turned on to a parallel course and Charles pointed at his tailplane. Alan waved back, trying to indicate that he had changed his mind, but Charles either misunderstood or decided to ignore the gesture, and turning sharply, settled his machine directly ahead of Alan's Avro. And much too close for comfort, Alan thought. Charles pointed to his tailplane, then turned away to port, expecting Alan to follow, and gesticulating wildly when he saw that Alan had made no attempt to do so.

Alan flew steadily on, Charles circling, climbing and diving around him, trying everything he knew to entice Alan into getting on his tail. Finally, cursing the blacksmith's plodding single-mindedness, he climbed high above the Avro and pushed his stick forward, determined at least to make Alan leave the straight and level course he was flying with such maddening persistence.

Alan looked back and saw the BE2 diving down at him. He was amused by Charles's capers. At the same time, he admired his friend's flying prowess. But not for long. As Alan watched the diving BE2 he had a sudden premonition of disaster. He felt certain that Charles was going to cut it even finer than he had done on his three previous dives. Yes, he was right! Charles was already closer than ever and there was no sign of his pulling out.

Alan kicked right rudder and shoved his stick forward in a diagonal movement, sending his Avro into a diving turn, glimpsing the BE2 as it shot past him, Charles's hand waving in wild triumph. The bloody fool! With savage determination Alan turned after Charles's machine, and for the next fifteen minutes clung grimly on to Charles's tail throughout a series of alarming manoeuvres.

'Bravo!' Charles cried, running up to the Avro as Alan taxied in. 'You see? Wasn't I right? You learn fast, don't you? Here, what's up?'

Alan did not speak until they reached his room, where he flung his helmet and goggles into his locker with uncharacteristic lack of care.

'That dive! You could have killed us both.'

Charles smiled blandly.

'That's our purpose *now*, isn't it? Killing, I mean. According to Captain Triggers, anyway.'

'He's teaching us to defend ourselves in the air.'

'He's some kind of a hero to you, of course.'

'Hardly that,' Alan said, quietly. 'But he did give me my chance to train as a pilot, don't forget. As for you—' He hesitated, not knowing quite how to put it. 'I'll feel the same, I expect, when it's my time to leave for France.'

Charles's face hardened.

'If you're implying that I've got the wind-up . . .'

'Don't talk rot!'

'All this business of killing. Shooting down Huns. I joined the Corps to fly. Not to kill.'

'So did I.'

'So did that Hun. The one Triggers and MacIver shot down as the poor devil was taking off. Just try putting yourself in his place. He couldn't have stood a chance.'

'They are the enemy, you know.'

'The Hun is also a fellow flier.'

Alan understood what Charles meant. There was a bond between all fliers regardless of race. The brotherhood of all who braved death in their flimsy, unreliable machines. Whether friend or foe, they shared a common danger. That was why they often exchanged waves with the Hun fliers; congratulatory gestures at their continuing triumph over death.

'With the occasional potshot now and then to keep us on

our toes, of course,' Alan said, smiling faintly. Then he looked more serious. 'But it can't go on like that, can it?'

'Not if chaps like Triggers have their way,' Charles retorted. 'No, we'll soon be slaughtering each other in the skies as they're doing on the ground.'

They looked at each other in silence for a moment. Alan was puzzled by Charles's view of Triggers. Alan was convinced that the man had their interests at heart. Charles shook his head, adamant in his opinion.

'I know his sort. I've met them in my regiment. Born for killing. Inspiring others to kill. Oh, my father would be greatly relieved to know that the Flying Corps has chaps like Triggers. My father will never forgive me for transferring from the regiment. To his way of thinking, I joined the RFC to duck my share of the killing.'

Alan started to pack his haversack. He felt certain now that MacIver was right. Charles was spoiling for a fight. And Alan had no desire to quarrel with his friend on this day of all days. He would not see Charles again for quite some time. The thought had occurred to him that he might never see him again; but he had pushed that from his mind.

'Perhaps you think that, too?' Charles said, truculently. Alan looked at him uncomprehendingly. 'That I joined the RFC to duck my share of the killing.'

'Who *wants* to kill?'

'*He* does!'

Alan blew impatiently and suggested they forget it. But Charles insisted on Alan's giving his opinion. On what?

'That Hun!'

'All this fuss over one German,' Alan hissed, striving to keep his temper. 'There are hundreds being killed every day in the trenches.'

'That's another matter. We're fliers! We're different! Surely you understand that?'

'I'm not sure that I do,' Alan said, quite genuinely. Oh yes, fliers had a code of honour, but as far as Alan was concerned – well – a man was a man, alive or dead, in the trenches or in the skies.

'Bravo!' Charles said with sarcastic admiration. Alan fastened his haversack in dogged silence. 'You condone it, then? That Hun! You'd do the same?'

'I don't know what I'd do. Or wouldn't do.'

'You mean you don't have a mind of your own?' He was goading Alan quite openly now. Alan commented that neither of them knew what it was like 'over there', so they couldn't honestly say what they might do or not do. 'You'd do anything Triggers would do. That's your trouble, Alan. You're so damned naïve.'

'*I'm* naïve?' Alan banged his haversack down on the bed. 'I like that. You're going to France tomorrow ...' He bit the words back.

'Do go on!' Charles entreated. 'Offering me advice?'

'All right, yes I am!' Alan flared. 'You go capering about over enemy lines like you did up there today – like a boy with a new toy – and the Hun will find you easy meat.'

Charles looked at him with icy disdain.

'I thought you might have understood,' he said. 'I should have known better. A blacksmith! You're just like MacIver. One can't expect chaps of your class to appreciate matters of honour and chivalry – and the proper conduct of gentlemen.'

They faced each other, both at white heat now. Alan picked up his haversack. Despite his anger, he stopped at the door to wish Charles 'Good luck', then cursed him all the way to Becket's Hill.

*

'Flying to France by himself,' Molly said, at tea. 'How will he find his way?'

'Compass and maps,' Alan said, wishing she would stop talking about Charles. Yes, he had said goodbye to him, and no, Charles's mother was not packing parcels for the Belgians. 'She doesn't actually pack them. She's on the committee. She helps to organize it.'

'The things women are doing,' Molly said. 'And there's me – four pairs of gloves and two scarves.'

'If it wasn't for you and others like you, the committees

would have nothing to put in their parcels, would they?' Harry said, quietly.

Molly looked heartened. As Alan was only home for one night, she had invited Lorna, Harry and Old Tom in to tea. Harry had put on his best suit and Lorna looked as if she had been grooming herself for a fortnight. Alan, who had been longing to see Lorna again, seemed almost unaware of her presence at the table, but she sensed that because he was in the company of the other men and wearing the uniform of which he was so proud, he was anxious not to appear mawkish. She understood that because she was trying so hard to hide her own feelings. Indeed, she was so conscious of the love shining in her eyes that she hardly raised them from the tablecloth until he passed her the bread and butter.

'Thank you,' she said, and if she had any doubts at all of Alan's feelings for her, his darting glance was enough to reassure her.

'Profit!' Tom said, suddenly, with everyone wondering what that had to do with anything said previously. 'That's all everyone thinks of these times. The wages they're paying to women at Claybourne's factory. It's scandalous. And not content any of them. Still wanting more by the hour.'

Molly gave a little uneasy smile in Harry's direction. She hoped Tom wouldn't start quarrelling with Harry. Not at a time like this. The two men always seemed to be at each other's throats lately. Harry wanted to put up the smithy's charges to meet the rising cost of living and Tom was in violent opposition. Molly agreed with Harry but she dare not antagonize Old Tom. Harry couldn't run the smithy with one arm and after all, Tom was the best smith in Sussex, everyone knew that.

'Did Charles have leave now he's going off to France?' Molly enquired, trying to change the subject.

'Yes, he did,' Alan replied. 'A farewell dinner at a Piccadilly restaurant. His mother and his sister.'

'Sister?' Lorna said, alertly, and then, realizing all eyes were upon her, tried to look disinterested. 'You didn't tell me Charles had a sister.'

'Didn't I? Well – he has.'

'A shortage of shells, they say,' Old Tom said, sternly, his eyes fixed on the cruet. 'Yet there's all this money being made in the factories. So there's something wrong somewhere, isn't there?'

'At the top, no doubt,' Harry said, casually. 'Things not being organized properly.'

'They want you there, eh?' Tom snapped. 'Telling them what to do.'

There was a short tense pause. Molly tried desperately to think of something to say.

'Even the smithies are after more money now,' Tom went on, disgustedly, ignoring Harry when he quietly commented that even blacksmiths had to eat. 'A fuss over the price they're paying for these shoes on the Government contract.'

'Quite right, too!' Harry said, curtly. 'We're losing money on those shoes, the price of iron and coal what it is. I think we should drop it.'

Old Tom looked appalled.

'What if all the smithies in the country did that?'

'We can't work at a loss.'

'You were in the cavalry. What would you have done without mounts?'

'Become infantry, I suppose,' Harry grinned.

Alan and Lorna laughed. Even Molly could not resist a smile. Old Tom looked black as thunder. 'Anyway, cavalry are done. Alan there – he's our cavalry now.'

'Have you met her?' Lorna asked. 'Charles's sister, I mean?'

'No, I haven't,' Alan said, remembering how stunningly beautiful the girl in the photograph had looked. 'Charles showed me her picture once.'

'What's her name?' Molly asked, beginning to regret having asked Tom in to tea.

'Kate.'

'That's a nice name,' Lorna said with a little forced smile.

'Prices are not our concern,' Tom growled across at Harry. 'You and me, that is.'

'True enough, Tom,' Harry said, with a good-natured smile.

'Our wages to be paid whether there's profit or no.'

'Profit! That's all people think of nowadays. The papers are full of it. The people drunk with it. There's more to life than profit.'

'We should know that if anyone does,' Harry said, philosophically. 'Our charges are still the same as in my father's day.'

'*Our* charges?' Tom said, challengingly. 'The missus here is the boss, remember. You left this place seventeen years ago, not caring tuppence.'

'Tom, please,' Molly remonstrated.

'Now you come back and want to run the place,' Tom went on.

'That's not true,' Molly said.

'You're not working with him. *I* am!' And the old man came to his feet. There was no stopping him now. He would have his say. And about time, too. 'Or working *for* him, rather. But that's a blacksmith's shop out there. It's not the army. Or a munitions factory.'

Harry had to smile.

'You're overdoing it, aren't you, Tom?'

'The boss out there is the smithy,' Tom shouted. 'Your brother Will understood that . . .'

'So do I, Tom . . .'

'I'll not be sergeant-farriered about. Nor speeded up. So! If you want to put up the charges and say what's what – then you'd better be smithy, too. In my place!' And he looked back at Molly from the door. 'I'm sorry, missus. But there it is.'

The long silence following Tom's stormy exit was broken by a sigh from Harry.

'Trust me to mess things up,' he said.

'Not your fault,' Molly said, cutting the cake she had baked for Alan's homecoming. 'We can't live on air.'

'We'll have a chance to find out very soon,' Harry said, ruefully. 'Who's going to be smithy out there now? I can't do the job – not with one arm.'

Alan was unusually silent as he walked Lorna back to the farm.

'How long will it be?' Lorna asked. 'Before you go to France?'

'It depends on how soon I—' He decided to rephrase it. 'How long it takes me to put my flying hours in.'

He was anxious to go, she knew that. She didn't mind; she understood how keen he was. But he looked troubled. Was it over Tom walking out like that?

'No. It's Charles. He's off to France tomorrow. We didn't part on the best of terms. And my fault. Because everything he said was right.'

Her eyes were moist. It concerned him. He slid his arms gently, protectively about her.

'It's all right,' she said, smiling up at him. 'It's just that I'm so proud of you, Alan. And I'm so lucky.'

He kissed her and drew her head on to his shoulder.

'You will take care, won't you?' she said, softly. And she held him tighter as a sudden fear gripped her. 'Take care . . .'

'Here,' he said, tenderly. 'It's Charles going off to France tomorrow. Not me.'

*

A group of lusty young singers, mostly trainee pilots, were singing an RFC Mess song when Charles arrived at the Blue Anchor. His heart sank when he saw Triggers seated at a table in the corner. Charles had been hoping that Triggers had forgotten his offer to buy him a farewell drink. But no such luck. And MacIver was there, too. Not exactly the two men Charles would have chosen for company on his last evening in England.

But Triggers was all smiles and good nature and as the evening wore on Charles found it difficult to believe that this same man had killed a Hun pilot in cold blood.

'We shot him down right enough,' MacIver said, when Triggers was at the bar ordering more drinks. 'Some'd play cards, you see. Or the three gramophone records. But not Triggers. He'd come over to the sergeants' Mess. Haul me out. Come on, he'd say – we'll go look for the Hun.'

'His pastime, eh? Hunting the Hun.'

'A particular Hun,' MacIver said, gazing morosely down at

the table. 'He'd got Paddy Walters, Triggers's observer. They were on fire. Going down in flames—'

'Gay Lion's off to France tomorrow,' Triggers said, putting the drinks on the table. 'He doesn't want to hear tales of woe, MacIver.'

Pearson came over from the piano.

'Excuse me, sir, but would you mind helping out?'

'Not tonight, Pearson.'

'But you're the only one who knows the words of the second verse, sir. Please, sir! Be a sport!'

'All right! But just the one verse.'

'Thank you, sir!'

Before he left the table, Triggers looked at Charles.

'Gay Lion,' he said, as if about to impart some great secret to Charles. 'Before you go tomorrow – I'll see you in B shed.'

And he went off to join the singers, leaving Charles filled with curiosity.

'I was telling you about his observer, Paddy Walters,' MacIver said, mournfully. 'This Hun shot them down in flames, you see. Triggers got out all right. But Paddy had been hit. And Triggers couldn't get to him.' He stared down at the table again as Charles waited for him to go on. 'Paddy was dead. That is – Triggers thought he was dead. But Paddy recovered consciousness just as the flames got to him.' He shook his head, looked as if he might cry, and coughed instead. 'There was nothing else Triggers could do.'

'What *did* he do?' Charles asked, wonderingly.

'As he told us this morning at that lecture – the forty-five has its uses.'

Charles stared at him.

'Triggers shot him?'

'Aye.' He sipped his beer. 'A terrible thing for a man to carry around in his mind, eh?'

'Was that the same Hun . . . ?'

'Aye. We went out looking for him for more than a week. But we didn't see a hair of him. Well, if he won't come out, Triggers said, then we'll make him come out. We flew over the Hun airfield. A hornets' nest. Everything shooting away at us.

I thought we were done for, I'll tell you. But he said we'd get that Hun. And we did.'

Charles looked at MacIver for a time, then across at the piano where Triggers was singing, loudly and boastfully, his eyes half closed, his arms draped around the shoulders of two young trainee pilots.

'He's a vengeful man,' MacIver said. And there was a warmth in his tone that might have come from the beer. 'But there's none better. I promise you that.'

The following afternoon, Charles started up his BE2, left MacIver in the cockpit, and waited in B shed as Triggers had asked him. Ten minutes went by and there was no sign of the man.

'We've given her a good warming up,' MacIver said, handing Charles a mug of steaming tea. 'She sounds really sweet.'

'Thanks. Triggers must have forgotten.'

'No, he hasn't. He's having a bit of trouble getting hold of one, that's all.'

'Getting hold of what?'

'Here he comes now.'

'There we are,' Triggers said, looking immensely pleased with himself. 'Just your size. I've gone to a lot of trouble to get this. We all had them when we flew to France.' And he held out the pumped-up inner tube to the gaping Charles. 'If you do come down in the Channel, at least it'll keep you afloat long enough.'

'Long enough . . . ?'

'To regret having ever left the cavalry.'

MacIver grinned and Charles felt ashamed of himself for ever having doubted Triggers's motives.

'Thank you, sir,' Charles said, sensing that Triggers knew what he was feeling.

'Good luck, Gay Lion.' Triggers said cheerily, but his face expressed mild concern as they watched Charles's machine taking off. 'We don't bat an eyelid, of course.'

'Pardon, sir?' MacIver blinked.

'When Sergeant Williams finds one of his back tyres missing.'

*

'They'll all take their business to the blacksmith's shop at Hopford,' Harry said, bleakly, as he cleaned out the hearth. 'We can't carry on here without a smithy and Tom knows it.'

'We'll manage somehow,' Molly said. 'And if we can't – well – I shan't blame you. You were right in saying we have to put our charges up. I was always telling Will that.' And she thought of Will's words: 'A blacksmith works to oblige and he's lucky if he makes a living as well.'

'Too soft Will was,' Harry commented.

'And you're the hard businessman, yes?' Molly smiled.

Harry put on a stony face and took the cup of tea she had brought him.

'It's no use hiding that account book from me,' he said. 'I took a look at it the day I started work here.'

'That why you won't take more than half a wage?' Molly said, gently.

He dare not look at her for fear she might suspect the deep love that was growing inside him.

'I don't need much,' he said, offhandedly. 'I've only myself to look after.'

Harry was lighting the smithy fire when Old Tom came in from the lane and stood there with his pipe in his mouth.

'You knew I'd turn up, eh?'

Harry hesitated, choosing his words carefully.

'I'm glad you have, I can tell you that.'

The old man came further into the smithy and stood there looking around the walls as if he had never seen them before.

'This damn place. I've been working here so long I've begun to think of it as my own. It's not! Belonged to your father. His father before him. So! You've a right to say how it's run.'

Harry felt a sudden wave of pity for the old man. He took out his pipe and tobacco.

'Alice had a go at me,' Old Tom went on. 'The way prices are going up, she said, I'll have to ask for more money soon.

And a fine fool I'll look then. How can they pay you more money if they don't put the charges up, she said.'

'Here, try a fill o' this,' Harry said. 'Horsetail shag we used to call it in the cavalry.'

They filled their pipes in silence, Harry searching for something to say that would make the old man feel easier, and in so doing, he found that he had revealed the truth of the situation to himself.

'Takes a bit of getting used to. Not having two hands. Watching others work with tools you once took a pleasure in using. Seems I've been taking it out on you, Tom. Making up for my lost arm with my tongue.'

Their eyes met. Harry took out his matches. Old Tom struck one and handed it to him.

'Ta!'

'It's women's tongues I can't abide,' Old Tom said. 'Though my Alice is right, I suppose. Still. You're wise, you know that? A man *is* better off on his own.'

'Maybe.'

'You don't sound too sure any more.' And the old man grinned. 'Don't tell me you got a secret love tucked away somewhere?'

Harry turned away to the hearth, the caged bird fluttering in his breast.

'The clinker in this last lot of coal from Evans,' he said. 'Just look at the size of that?'

'It ruins the work,' Tom growled. 'In the old days we'd have had him off the cart and beat the coal dust out of his bones. Things are different now.'

Not much different, Harry mused, smiling inside at the fanciful thoughts of love in the head of that foolish young man who had left Becket's Hill with a broken heart to join the Army. Yet now, here he was, supposedly older and wiser, feeling much the same again. Damn and bless the woman! He would always love Molly Grayson. He knew that for certain now. Whether or not he would ever tell her ... that was another matter.

*

Alan looked crestfallen when MacIver told him that Charles had left no message.

'He was cheerful enough,' MacIver said. Then he gave a grudging smile. 'He's not such a bad feller, I suppose. As officers go.'

He was much more than that, Alan thought, as he climbed into the Avro, and he was more impatient than ever to get his posting to France. He wanted desperately to apologize to Charles for his angry words. Charles had been a good friend to him during those early days when they had taken their tickets together. Alan had been acutely aware of his own humble background whilst having to mix with commissioned officers and sons of 'the gentry' to which he had been brought up to touch his cap, and Charles's friendship and easy-going nature had helped Alan to feel less of a fish-out-of-water. Anyway, Charles had been right; they had joined the Corps to fly, not to kill.

'Switch on!'

'Switch on!'

'Contact!'

The Avro leapt forward, bounded over the grass, and roared towards the trees at the far end of the field. As always, in these moments when the trees were directly ahead, Alan saw his father trying to free his legs from the tangled wreckage of The Flyer in the tree at the bottom of Collins's field.

Suddenly, the engine started spluttering. Alan immediately eased the stick forward to reduce the angle of climb, Triggers's warning words reverberating in his mind: 'Never turn back – get your nose down to maintain flying speed and look for a suitable place to land.' Alan's eyes were already scanning the countryside ahead as he prayed for the spluttering to stop. It did! And all he could hear was the wind in the struts and bracing wires.

'He's got his nose down, anyway.' Triggers blew relievedly, jumped down from the Farman and sprinted to the gates where the Crossley tender had just turned in, its engine still running. 'Turn around and go like hell.'

Triggers's eyes were glued to the Avro as the tender sped

along the lane. Crash landings were arduous enough for old hands at the game and tested one's skill to its limits; for these young trainee pilots it was a fifty-fifty chance of a crash landing, and that meant a fifty-fifty chance of survival.

The Avro disappeared from view beyond a tall hedge and Triggers waited tensely for the sound of the crash. He heard nothing above the sound of the Crossley's engine.

'Turn left here,' he shouted to the driver. Then he saw the sheet of orange flame and the cloud of black smoke. He vaulted the stile and ran, heavy-footed, over the ploughed earth to the blazing machine. In his mind he could hear the screams of Paddy Walters, his observer, just before he had taken out his revolver and shot him through the head. He stopped just short of the burning Avro and looked wildly around. There was no sign of Farmer. 'Farmer? Where the hell are you?'

Protecting his face from the heat, Triggers ran closer to the hellish blaze, stopping short as he glimpsed Alan through the flames. He was standing on the far side of the burning machine, his face bleeding from cuts on both cheeks.

'What's the matter? Are you deaf or what?'

Alan looked at him dazedly and said he was sorry.

'Sorry? Sorry for what?' Thank Christ the lad was alive. 'I thought you were frying in there.'

'I made a mistake, sir. The biggest mistake of all. I forgot to switch off.'

Triggers was stone-faced.

'You're all right then?'

'Yes, sir. Thank you, sir.'

'Just your observer who's frying in there.'

His tone was harsh, and Alan, numb with the shock of his narrow escape from dying in the same horrifying manner as his father had done, did not understand the significance of Triggers's words. Then, as he watched Triggers staring into the flames, the 'message' sank in.

'Your observer's life is in your hands,' Triggers said solemnly as they walked to the tender. 'Just remember that when you get to France.'

chapter eleven

Harry walked to the end of Haverton Lane, stared into the distance down Leadby Street, winked at the two boys who were already waving their Union Jacks, and went back into the smithy. He was surprised to find Molly there.

'Do I look smart enough?' she asked, anxiously putting up her hands to adjust the brim of her hat.

'Very smart,' Harry said, stifling the voice inside him that yearned to tell her that no one had ever looked more beautiful. 'No sign of the car yet.'

'Plenty of time though, isn't there?'

'Aye. Plenty of time.'

They exchanged slight, formal smiles, in the way that people do when the time for parting with a loved one draws near.

'I can't really believe he's going,' Molly said. And she laughed, lightly. 'Silly, isn't it? It seems no time at all since he joined up.' She turned away, staring at the ashes in the forge with unseeing eyes. 'As he says, there are hundreds of others going.'

Harry nodded, thinking of the time she and Will had seen him to the station when he had gone off to join the cavalry all those years ago. Now they were seeing her son off to France.

'It was good of Colonel Starke to offer to drive us to the station,' Molly said. And she looked so appealingly at Harry that it was all he could do to stop himself putting his arm about her shoulders to comfort her. 'I mustn't make a fool of myself. Not in front of the Colonel.'

In the kitchen, Lorna was fastening the straps of his haversack when Alan came downstairs.

'I've put your sandwiches in,' she said. 'Don't forget to write.'

'I won't.'

They stood there looking at each other in silence. She was proud of him, despite anything else she was feeling. The sergeant's stripes and propellers on his sleeves, and on his left breast, the coveted 'wings'.

'When I do get leave,' Alan said, not knowing quite how to put it, 'I've been thinking. Perhaps we ought to make things more definite between us. That's if you agree . . .'

'Oh yes,' she said breathlessly. 'Yes, I do.'

He came over to her, held her gently, and kissed her.

'It's funny,' he said. 'I've been waiting impatiently all this time to be posted to France. Now I don't want to go. Because it means leaving you. I have to be honest. I hadn't considered that important before. And I'm not just saying it to make it easier for you.'

Her eyes brimmed with tears but her heart was singing with joy.

'I know that,' she said. 'You never say anything you don't mean.'

'I love you, Lorna.'

'I love you, too, Alan.'

He leaned forward to kiss her again, but before his lips met hers there was a rap on the door and Molly came in, Harry just behind her.

'The Colonel's motor car is on its way.'

They all stood there, not knowing what to say next.

'Tom's gone over for Alice,' Molly said. 'You've got your sandwiches?'

'In the haversack,' Lorna said.

'You won't forget the bed?' Molly said, anxiously.

'Bed?'

'They say it's very damp over there.'

'Not now,' Alan murmured. Mothers were embarrassing at times. 'It's June, very near.'

Old Tom rapped and came in.

'Alice won't come over. She'll wave from the window. She's a bit upset. Natural. She was always fond of Alan.'

That was all Molly needed. She had to turn away to straighten the brass horse on the mantelshelf.

'You're off at last, then,' Tom said. 'You'll give them what for, eh?'

'Maybe,' Alan murmured.

'Harry been off to two wars,' the old man went on. 'Now you off to one. And there's me – seventy-two and never heard a shot fired in anger. A fine thing to tell a son – if I had one.' There was a fond gleam in his eye now. 'You're the nearest I've had to a son, Alan. So. Look after yourself, eh?'

'I will, Tom.'

And they shook hands.

'Goodbye, lad.'

*

The front lines were only six or seven miles away and Alan could hear the pounding of the big guns as the Crossley tender jolted down the cart track, the ruts from the winter's mud already drying hard in the warm May sun. They trundled through a farmyard, hens clucking and fluttering, and a bitter-faced farmer scowling as the tender shaved the wheel of his passing cart.

'We're not too popular, o' course,' the driver grinned. 'Our machines crash-landing on their crops and frightening the animals. I think the French farmers hate the Flying Corps more than they do the Boche. Here we are. St Marie airfield right in front of you.'

Alan saw nothing but a row of poplars looming up into the blue sky. Then, as they turned off the track through a pair of rotting gate posts, he saw the row of tents and a sign nailed to a tree stump: 'Paddington Mews'.

'NCOs and other ranks. The officers are billeted in Hyde Park Mansions.' The driver nodded towards the large barn. 'You'll find the flight offices there, too. Not quite what you expected, eh? I know. The Flying Corps, you sometimes think you're not really in the war at all. You'll soon know different, they say, once you fly over enemy lines.'

Alan took his kitbag, haversack and greatcoat from the back, and as the tender trundled off he stood there surveying the scene. On the far side of the field, two men were tugging at a large T-shaped piece of canvas. The wind had veered and they were adjusting it so that the longer section of the landing-T pointed into the wind. One of the occupants of Paddington Mews was seated on the grass cleaning his rifle and a rigger was patching bullet-holes in the fuselage of a BE2 situated in front of the Bessonneau hangar. The guns had stopped now and all was peaceful and still. Standing there, alone in a foreign land, ignored and unwelcomed, Alan felt an acute sense of disappointment. He had been so looking forward to his first glimpse of the Squadron with which he was going to fly as an operational pilot. After three days at the Aircraft Depot, awaiting his posting in a continued state of suppressed excitement, the OC's words 'You're being sent to St Marie' had become synonymous with feverish activity, brave-faced camaraderie and the myriad small urgencies of a makeshift wartime flying field. But looking around at the hazy stillness of the broad French countryside and smelling the particular air of apathetic peace that hung like a cloud over 'St Marie', Alan felt he might well have been back in miles-away-from-the-war Becket's Hill.

He decided not to knock on the door marked 'Hyde Park Mansions' and walked further along to the one marked 'C Flight Office'.

'Come in!'

As he entered the office, Alan suffered the same shiver of apprehension that he had felt on the day of his interview at the War Office.

'Sergeant Farmer, is it?'

'Yes, sir. Posted from St Omer.'

'Just over from Blighty, eh?' The officer at the desk drummed his fingers as he looked at the chessmen on a board in front of him. He was about twenty-four, rather too good-looking, and at this moment, sourly reflective. He had barely glanced at Alan when he came in. 'Thirteen hours' flying time, I'm told. That's a jolly little number to send you over with.'

Alan swallowed, not sure if he was supposed to smile or not. The officer continued to pore over his chessmen. The stillness outside seemed to have pervaded the office and Alan shuffled uncomfortably, wondering what to say next.

'I was told to report to the Adjutant.'

'He's out on a raid.'

Alan looked suitably impressed.

'Looking for a piano for the Mess,' he added. 'You're in 'C' Flight. I'm your Flight-Commander, Captain Dornish.'

Alan stood even more stiffly to attention.

'What were you before?' Dornish enquired, languidly, as if he didn't much care. 'Mechanic, observer, or what?'

'I was a blacksmith, sir.'

Dornish lost interest in the chessmen.

'A blacksmith? My, we *are* getting desperate for chaps, aren't we? How many times have you crashed?'

'Just the once, sir.'

That was something, anyway. But how many times had his engine failed, and bits of his machine fallen off in the air?

'You see what I mean? Our machines are a dangerous enemy in themselves, without Hun batteries and machine-guns potting away at us. Thirteen hours? Good God, man, you need fifty at least before flying over enemy lines.' He sounded as if it were all Alan's fault and nodded irritably to a walking-stick hanging on the back of a chair, asking Alan to hand it to him. 'You know what we do here, I suppose?'

'Ranging for the artillery, sir,' Alan said, trying hard not to stare at the stiff leg as Dornish limped over to the map on the wall.

'A nice soft job. As any infantryman will tell you. You circle the target, listening to your own artillery shells whistling past, while enemy Archie blasts away at you. Thought you were training to be an eagle, did you? I'll tell you now, you're a sitting duck. And with a jolly rotten set of feathers.' He pointed to the map with his stick. 'That's us. St Marie. The two batteries we're ranging for are here – and here. You won't know the Clock Code, of course . . .'

Alan coughed politely and said that he did. He had taken the trouble to pick it up from Sergeant MacIver back at Beechwood. Again, Dornish looked mildly surprised. He handed Alan a circular celluloid disc marked with concentric circles and numbered on its circumference like a clock. He posed a ranging problem, indicating a theoretical target on the map.

'You see the shell exploding here. What correction will your observer signal to the ground battery?'

Alan placed the disc on the map with the centre spot over the target, straightened the north-south line and noted that the 'shellburst' was on the concentric circle marked B and that the clock number of that particular section was nine.

'B nine, sir.'

Dornish smiled for the first time.

'I imagine you made some jolly fine horseshoes,' he said. 'Come on! Paddington Mews!'

The tent smelled of grass and dirty socks.

'They're little ponds of hell in the winter. In the summer, they're not too bad. Except for the earwigs. But being a country lad, you'll feel quite at home, eh?'

There were two canvas cots, one with rumpled blankets, a half-written letter, a copy of *Flight* and half a bar of chocolate.

'Sergeant Merrigold. He's working with number two battery this morning.' He saw Alan looking at the framed photograph hanging on the tent-pole. A most attractive young woman. 'Believe it or not – it's his mother.'

A Mess orderly entered with two mugs of coffee on the lid of a tin box serving as a tray. Dornish made a face.

'Ugh! Still no milk?'

'Afraid not, sir. Sorry.'

'A stray shell demolished the dairy along with two adjoining cottages,' Dornish explained. 'That's where the Adjutant is hopefully rescuing a piano for us.' He watched Alan dutifully sipping his coffee. 'Awful, isn't it? Well, Farmer, I've some good news for you. My leg's beginning to thaw out so I shall be flying again tomorrow. I got you here on the strength of this leg. We're so short of chaps we're not allowed spare pilots. But you will be spare now. So make the most of it. Live in the air for the next week or so. Get to know our sector like your girlfriend's eyebrows.'

'Yes, sir. I will, sir.' He was beginning to like Captain Dornish.

'Only one snag. There's no machine for you.' He blinked thoughtfully at Alan's disappointment. 'Anyway, for today, you can use mine.'

'Thank you, sir.'

'I hear you're rather handy with engines.'

'Yes, I am, sir,' Alan said, with a touch of pride.

'Tinker with mine on pain of death,' Dornish said, sharply. 'And for Heaven's sake stay well on our side of the lines. It so happens we've got a Hun who's making rather a nuisance of himself.'

The German observer was equipped with a Parabellum machine-gun. The pilot had spotted the BE2 flying several thousand feet below and as he turned to bring his machine on to a parallel course, his observer prepared to fire downwards on the port beam.

Lieutenant Bravington, a phlegmatic, fair-haired bear of a man, whose bodyweight further reduced the BE2's poor rate of climb, had noted the shellburst, worked out the code correction, and now picked up the lamp to signal to the ground battery. This was the part of the job that he loathed. He had to turn around in the cockpit – no mean feat for a man of his size – and then lean well aft to clear the obstructing lower wing or the morse signal would not be seen. He struggled to a kneeling position on the seat, almost dropping the lamp over the side and mentally denting the skull of the BE2's designer with the blasted thing. Why they had not considered putting the controls and the pilot in the front cockpit was utterly beyond his reasoning. If he had been sitting in Sergeant Merrigold's cockpit he would have had a much clearer view of the ground below and he would not have had to go through this damned contortionist's palaver every time he needed to signal to a battery that was obviously going to take the best part of the morning to hit that bloody supply dump.

He had just begun the signal when he heard a sound like the Devil's engine starting up. Chunk-chunk-chunk-chunk ... He threw the lamp into the cockpit and reached for his Winchester in the rack, his eyes already scanning for the Hun. The

Albatross was above him, on the starboard beam, the German observer traversing the Parabellum; a black-clad harbinger of death. Chunk-chunk-chunk-chunk ... Sergeant Merrigold, shouting something Bravington could not possibly hear, slumped forward in his cockpit. The BE2 lurched forward. Bravington, sliding from his kneeling position on the seat, grabbed the cockpit rim to prevent himself falling out, the butt of his Winchester catching him a glancing blow on the head as it fell from his grasp and went spinning slowly through space.

'Merrigold'! he bawled, but there was no response. He clambered out of his cockpit and clawed his way back to the pilot. 'Merrigold! Damn you!'

But Merrigold was dead. Or unconscious, at least. His bent head slid slowly along the rim of the cockpit of the spiralling machine. Bravington pushed the head roughly back and felt around inside the cockpit, trying to find the throttle lever. Though he didn't know why. He was plunging to certain death. Cutting the engine would only prolong the dreadful moments of waiting. He was helpless. That was the observer's lot. If your pilot was killed you had no chance at all. There was nothing you could do. Except jump! That way, at least, you avoided the possibility of cremation. But it took courage to jump. More courage than he had at this time. He found the throttle lever and pulled it upwards. The engine stopped. The machine was still spiralling to earth but with much less urgency. Death was moving towards him now, sooner than rushing to greet him, but the meeting was just as inevitable.

'Merrigold, for Christ's sake!'

He reached further into the cockpit, feeling for the control lever. Damn it! Merrigold's hand was still gripping it; holding it firmly in the forward position. If only he could manage to centralize the lever ... he caught hold of Merrigold's sleeve and tugged.

The BE2 curved upwards and Bravington shoved his knees into the back of his own cockpit to prevent himself sliding down the length of fuselage. Talk about a bloody circus. This was crazy! What the hell was he doing? Why couldn't he face death like a man instead of trying to slide away from it like a gibbering coward? He still had hold of Merrigold's sleeve. With his other hand, he grabbed the control lever, or rather, Merrigold's hand, which was still gripping it quite firmly. The hand moved, and suddenly Merrigold's eyes were open and staring into Bravington's. Almost crying with relief, Bravington inched his way back to his own cockpit, his eyes fixed on Merrigold, who looked over the side with glazed eyes seeking the familiar landmarks that would enable him to make his turn for 'home'.

Alan had resolved to do something about the Squadron's lack of fresh milk and was just climbing the stile into the field of cows when he heard the approaching BE2. He sat there enjoying the thrill of his first sight of a returning operational machine, then carried on into the field.

The BE2 taxied to the hangar and stopped. Merrigold, glassy-eyed but smiling faintly, raised a thumb in weak triumph.

'Well done, old son!' Bravington fumbled for the brandy flask beneath his flying coat, unscrewed the cap and put it to Merrigold's lips. Merrigold gulped, a strange noise in his throat. His head lolled back and his eyes stared sightlessly up at the sky.

'Good old Adjutant!' Charles Gaylion cried when he found the battered old piano in the Mess lounge. 'Here goes! "Mysterious Rag"!'

'Good God, do all French pianos sound like that?' James Favell said, listening in utter incredulity to the off-key sounds emerging from the open top of the instrument.

'You'd sound like that if you'd been blown through a cottage wall,' Charles replied gaily. Since leaving England, two months ago, his fingers had been itching to play and he was thoroughly enjoying himself.

'Coffee, sir?' the Mess orderly enquired.

'No thanks,' Charles said, with a significant shake of the head.

'Here, hang on,' Favell cried, looking in amazement at the jug on the orderly's tray. 'There's milk!'

'Lord! So there is!'

'Adjutant must have found us another dairy.'

'No, sir. It's the new pilot. He milked one of the cows across the way.'

Charles and Favell exchanged looks.

'Now why didn't *we* think of that?' Charles said.

'A genius in our midst,' Favell said, sipping his coffee with drooling delight. 'Here, we ought to welcome the chap. He's in our Flight, after all.'

'What's his name, do you know?' Charles asked the orderly.

'Farmer, sir. Sergeant Farmer.'

Charles stared at the orderly. Favell grimaced.

'Not another sergeant pilot, surely?' Favell didn't believe in this business of chaps coming up through the ranks to be made pilots. Working-class chaps. A lot of them were jolly good mechanics but they weren't really the proper chaps to have command of an aeroplane. And you never got to know them sufficiently well enough to establish a good working relationship in the air.

'Not a blacksmith, is he?' Charles enquired.

'I've no idea, sir. He's in Paddington Mews. Sergeant Merrigold's tent.'

A corporal was putting Sergeant Merrigold's belongings into a kitbag and Bravington was making an inventory of his personal effects when Charles burst into the tent. Bravington scowled and Charles apologized when he saw what they were doing.

'Sergeant Merrigold! Rotten luck. No one said.'

'Like us to go round with a megaphone?' Bravington said, acidly.

'What happened?'

'Our favourite Hun.' Bravington looked across at Alan's bed. 'The new pilot. Thirteen hours, they tell me. He was supposed to be a spare man.'

Charles took the photograph of Merrigold's mother from the tent-pole and handed it to Bravington, who sighed sharply

161

and went out, the corporal following with the kitbag. Charles looked at Alan's bed-space, smiling to himself at the order and neatness of it all. The blacksmith was a methodical chap.

Returning from lunch in the sergeants' Mess, Alan's delight on seeing Charles again was clouded by the memory of the harsh words they had exchanged on the occasion of their last meeting on the day before Charles left for France.

'It seems that our lives are inextricably intertwined,' Charles said. 'As they say in all the best novels. You're in 'C' Flight then? So am I.'

'How long have you been at St Marie?'

'Six weeks. Ever since I came over.'

'I'm a spare pilot.'

Charles glanced instinctively at Merrigold's bed and Alan now became aware that Merrigold's belongings had been taken away.

'Sergeant Merrigold moved out?'

'You could say that, I suppose,' Charles said, quietly.

Alan thought he understood.

'I'm no longer a spare chap then?'

'There's a hell of a lot to learn, you know,' Charles said, remembering his own first trip over enemy lines and feeling sorry for Alan, who was obviously going to be thrown in at the deep end. It was a busy time and every man in the Squadron was flying every day. 'Oh, you think you know it all when you first arrive. I know I did.'

They were conscious again of their last meeting in England.

'The day before you left for France,' Alan said, 'I as good as called you a coward.'

'And you were right. We all are. You find it out the first time you fly over the Hun lines.' He smiled at Alan's disbelief, then recalled his own words on the occasion of their last meeting. 'I said that as you were a blacksmith, you'd know nothing of the conduct of gentlemen.'

'We were both angry at the time,' Alan said, with an awkward smile.

'The surprising thing is – out here, the most extraordinary chaps turn out to be gentlemen.' And Charles glanced at Sergeant Merrigold's bed. 'It has very little to do with manners or the cut of a chap's clothes.'

They were silent for a time.

'Captain Dornish has kindly lent me his machine to take my first look around,' Alan said, taking his flying gear from his kitbag.

'I'll come with you.'

'There's no need . . .'

'Oh yes, there jolly well is. You've got some cramming to do. You'll need your eyes for a hundred and one things down there on the ground. That's when chaps get caught out. And we've got a brand new Hun – with a machine-gun.'

They flew east of Bethune, Alan marvelling at the soft colours of the French countryside that looked so enchanting despite the scars of war, the breadth of it all so utterly foreign to him, and yet, hardly a giant stone's throw away from the cosiness of the English landscape. And the straightness of the roads. The military precision of the lines of poplars. Even the waters looked different somehow; the afternoon sun gleaming on the knife-blade canal, piercing La Bassée. To the north, the coastline was shrouded in a delicate mist, and Alan's mind wafted through it, flew swiftly on, across the Channel and the English coast to Becket's Hill, his mother baking the bread for Sunday and Lorna herding the cows in for milking.

They puttered around the sector for two hours, Charles scanning watchfully, his Winchester at the ready, and pointing out the important features, including the two gun batteries Alan would be working with and the emergency landing ground used by the Squadron when a machine had run out of fuel, suffered engine failure, or for one of a dozen other reasons was unable to make the flight home to St Marie on returning from a gruelling reconnaissance trip deep into the hostile air beyond the enemy lines.

Alan thrilled at his first glimpse of front line trenches, the orange flashes of the big guns, and the puffs of black smoke that suddenly appeared in the hazy air and faded just as magically.

'It's thrilling enough watching it all from our side of the

lines, maybe,' Charles said, as he climbed out of the cockpit. 'It's a different kettle of fish when you're watching it from the other side.'

'I'll bet,' Alan said, flushed with the excitement of being fired upon by British 'Archie' soon after they had turned back from the front lines. 'I can't wait to go on my first trip.'

'It may well be sooner than you think,' Charles said, grimly.

Favell was winding up the gramophone when Charles breezed into the Mess lounge that evening.

'Flight meeting in half an hour.'

'The long reconnaissance again, I'll bet,' Favell said, glumly.

'Yes, it is. I heard from Sergeant Mills in the office. Three machines. Us, Connolly and Captain Dornish.'

'Our Flight-Commander back in harness again, eh?' Favell grinned. 'I hope his leg stiffens up. We'll spend half the morning circling the airfield and it'll be too late to go.'

Dornish was playing chess with Bravington.

'I'm quite impressed with Sergeant Farmer, the new chap,' Dornish said. Bravington nodded, indifferent, his eyes on the chessboard. 'He'd already taken the trouble to learn the Clock Code.' He smiled pleasantly as Bravington's eyes narrowed with suspicion. 'Brigade sent their congrats on your morning's work, by the way.'

'I'll pass them on to Sergeant Merrigold,' Bravington said. dourly. 'What else did Brigade say?'

'That hostile battery you spotted. They'd like to knock it out.' He lit his pipe for the third time. 'Tomorrow.'

Bravington's features hardened.

'Can't be done, can it? Three pilots. All on the long reconnaissance.'

Dornish moved his bishop.

'I've already mentioned it to Sergeant Farmer. He's very keen.'

Bravington seethed in silence for a time.

'Why do I always get the new ones?' he snapped.

'You are the best observer on the Squadron.'

That didn't make sense to Bravington. The best observer, yet it seemed he was the most expendable.

'I'd have thought in that case you'd want to hang on to me.'

'A new chap,' Dornish said, offhandedly. 'His first time over enemy lines and only fifteen hours in his book. Nice to know he's in good hands, as it were.'

That didn't make sense to Bravington, either.

'I've got it wrong, of course. I thought it was the other way round. That my life was in *his* hands.'

Dornish appeared to be more interested in the dampness of his tobacco.

'Nice enough chap for a sergeant,' he said, lighting up once again. 'He's a blacksmith.'

That was all Bravington needed to know.

'I see. Heavy hands at that.'

Alan was wrapping two spark-plugs and a pair of pliers into a handkerchief when Bravington came into the tent. He stood stiffly to attention as Bravington introduced himself.

'I thought we might have a chat.'

'Yes, sir. Spark-plugs and pliers, sir. In case our engine fails.'

Bravington nodded gravely. Engine failure with a new pilot was not exactly the jolliest of thoughts. Alan, for his part, was anxious to assure his senior officer that he was pretty good at repairing engines. Bravington blinked. Was the chap showing off or what?

'And I've drawn a fusee canister from the stores, sir.' Alan displayed the small leather cylinder with the brass lid. 'We do burn our machine if there's any chance of capture, don't we, sir?'

'Let's not look for troubles, eh?' Bravington said, his tone heavy with foreboding. 'I've got enough on my plate as it is.'

'Sorry, sir.'

He was still standing keenly to attention. Bravington gave a pained look and nodded wearily at Alan's bed. Alan thanked him and sat down, noting Bravington's unease as the other man sat down on Sergeant Merrigold's bed.

'I was sorry to hear about Sergeant Merrigold, sir. I understood you were flying with him when it happened.'

Bravington did not reply. He had been so close to death that morning he still found it hard to believe that he was actually alive; at various times during the day he had stopped to ask himself if it was really Richard Bravington still eating, breathing and talking. He unfolded the map and showed Alan the position of the hostile battery they proposed to knock out on the following morning.

'The guns we're working with are just here.'

'Yes, sir. Number two battery. I took a look at it this afternoon. I went up with Mr Gaylion. How do they indicate when they're ready to fire, sir?'

'They lay out strips of cloth with the code lettering.'

Alan looked impressed.

'Oh yes, it's all very well organized,' Bravington went on. 'But nine times out of ten it ends up in an unholy waste of time for all concerned. Sometimes you can't see the code lettering. So you go down to take a closer look and some idiot fires on you. Or you find the hostile battery you're after has moved and you try to signal back and they mistake it for the signal to fire and just miss blasting you out of the sky. Or some other battery starts firing who hadn't been warned that yours was going to fire, or . . .' He stopped, smiling faintly at Alan's shattered expression. 'But let's forget the damned hostile battery for a moment, shall we? Let's talk about the important thing.'

'What's that, sir?'

'Our wheels touching down on the field out there when we return. It's a good feeling, I can tell you.'

Alan nodded slowly, understanding how Bravington felt. An experienced man placing his life in the hands of a raw beginner. He didn't know what to say. He'd liked to have told him he was confident enough but that might have sounded 'cocky'.

'You know about enemy, Archie?'

'Yes, sir. I had a taste of our own this afternoon. It was misty, so they couldn't have seen my roundels.'

'They don't look too hard, I warn you. White puffs?'

'Yes, sir.'

'The Hun's are black. Hell of a noise. High explosive. As soon as you see one – start weaving.'

'Yes, sir.'

'Now. The Hun. On the whole, he's quite a decent chap. Doesn't bother us too much. But we've got a brand new one – who does.'

'Yes, sir, I've heard. With a machine-gun.'

'We've a rifle and revolver! And the Hun flies higher and faster than we do.' He gave Alan a moment to allow that to sink in, then posed the question. 'So what do we do?' Alan looked uncertain. 'We don't take any chances, that's what. A speck of that Hun and we turn for home.' And a little reminder, just in case. 'That's west, by the way.'

'Yes, sir.'

'Normally, the Hun won't give chase. He doesn't fly on our side of the lines.'

'Why not?'

'Because he's a sensible chap.' And there was a touch of bitterness in his voice now. 'Obeying orders of superior officers who realize the value of their men and their machines.' In high contrast to the Flying Corps, who appeared to Bravington to be an ill-organized amateur suicide club. 'However, *if* the Hun should decide to give chase – the one thing never to do is to lose height. The Hun already has a height advantage with a machine that flies higher than ours. So you don't give him another inch. Understood?'

'Yes, sir.'

Alan did not sleep a wink that night. He rose at four, lit the lamp, and meticulously cleaned and checked his Webley-Scott revolver. It was still dark outside when Second Class Air Mechanic Miller, a ginger cockney, pushed his head through the tent flap.

'Any more for the Skylark? Breakfast is ready in fifteen minutes, sarge. Good luck your first time over.'

In the Mess, two sergeant pilots from 'A' Flight also wished him luck, and Alan glowed with the warmth of comradeship and pride in the importance of his task as he put on his flying coat and helmet.

Outside the Bessonneau hangars, the dark air throbbed with the concerted roar of engines running-up. Mechanics and riggers ghosted about in the misty half-light, yawning in greasy pyjamas, cursing for spanners, complaining about the dew and some silly bugger who had put a mug of steaming tea down on the grass.

'My feet are not so bloody cold I want 'em scalded.'

Lieutenant Bravington felt like death itself as he attached his map to the clipboard. He'd been damned lucky. Three new pilots on the trot and he'd survived them all. But only just! And his luck had to run out some time. He still hadn't got over his shattering experience of the previous day. On top of that, he had a hell of a hangover; the result of trying to obliterate all thoughts of what today held in store for him.

'Don't damned well forget,' he snapped bad-temperedly as Alan wished him good morning. 'If we *are* attacked by a Hun – don't lose height.'

Alan performed his worst take-off ever, skimming the top of 'B' Flight hangar. He could not hear the words, but Bravington mouthed them with such fierce precision that no one could have failed to mistake them.

'Christ All bloody Mighty!'

Alan was now so intent on proving to Bravington that he was *not* the worst pilot in the Corps that he forgot all about the poplars just beyond the hangar, and as they loomed out of the mist he had to yank the stick sharply back to avoid hitting the tops. Bravington glared at him, long and hard, convinced that his life had been placed in the hands of a stone-blind, uncoordinated, anvil-thumping halfwit, and he pointed a dictatorial finger in the direction of the gun battery they were to work with that morning and kept it pointing until Alan had completed the turn and their machine was correctly headed on its course.

The first shellburst was north of the target. Bravington worked out the code correction and reached for the lamp to signal to the battery. As he twisted around in his seat, he waved to Alan to turn to starboard. Alan had just begun the turn when there was a blinding flash on the port side, just above him, and as he hurtled across the sky he heard an appalling bang. He saw Bravington hanging on grimly with one hand and waving like fury with the other. He realized he had just had first taste of the Hun Archie fire and that Bravington was telling him to 'get weaving'. He kicked left rudder and pushed the stick over and they went careering into a tight left-hand turn. Bravington threw his lamp back into the cockpit, glaring and cursing everything and everyone; the new pilot, the RFC, the whole ridiculous idea of using aeroplanes in warfare. Blast the Wright brothers for ever inventing this absurd death-trap. Why the hell couldn't they stick to repairing bicycles?

Acrid black smoke stung Alan's nostrils as he turned sharply in the opposite direction and in his mind's eye he saw the smoke rising above the elm trees on that Saturday afternoon when his father had burned to death. A second explosion, just as close, but below them this time, lifted the machine as if an airborne mule had kicked it in the belly. Three more explosions rocked the machine as Alan turned her from side to side, then Bravington picked up the lamp and held up his hand, indicating to Alan to fly straight and level. Alan peered over the side, his eyes scouring the countryside below. Where the hell was the battery? In his panic he had lost all sense of direction. He looked at Bravington. The man's face was a mask of hatred as he waved to Alan to turn to port, holding up his hand at the moment to stop the turn and to fly straight and level once again. Alan felt like a puppet, miserably incompetent, and he remembered Sergeant MacIver's words back at Beechwood: 'The observer's the important chap. The pilot is just a chauffeur.' And quite obviously, in Bravington's eyes, Alan was a bloody awful chauffeur at that.

Bravington finished making the signal and pointed in the direction of the target. As Alan made the turn a phrase kept repeating itself over and over in his mind. 'Never turn back, never turn back, never turn back ...' and he knew now that the queasiness he felt stemmed not from the fear of death but the fear of making mistakes. His father had made a fatal

169

mistake in turning back to Collins's field on that awful Saturday afternoon three years ago and had caused Alan's mother untold suffering and grief. In obeying some vague compulsion that he could not quite rationalize, Alan felt he was atoning for his father's mistake by never making one himself. He recalled how proud he had been of his reputation at Beechwood; the only pupil who had not crashed a machine. And how miserable he had been on the day he had crash-landed and burned his machine by forgetting to switch off. It was odd that the mistake itself should concern him more than the narrow escape from the horrible result of it.

The second battery shell was even further off target than the first and Bravington glowered at Alan as if he was entirely to blame. The third shell was closer. As Bravington worked out the correction, Alan caught sight of a menacing speck approaching from the east. A Hun! His first instinct was to carry out Bravington's firm instruction of the night before; to turn west immediately and fly for home. But he stubbornly rejected this for two very good reasons. Firstly, Bravington was only seconds away from making the signal to the battery that might result in the next shell destroying the target, and Alan desperately wanted to return to St Marie secure in the knowledge that his first task over enemy lines had been successfully accomplished. Secondly, he had been a puppet quite long enough. He wasn't just a chauffeur; he had a mind of his own and he could use it. Then he realized that he had a third reason, of course. The most important one perhaps. He had to prove his true worth to Bravington before the day was out.

Bravington, for some reason, took longer than usual to work out the code correction, and as Alan watched the rapidly approaching Hun he hoped to God Bravington wouldn't spot it before he made the signal.

Bravington looked over the side to the position of the previous shellburst. Alan looked quickly away from the Hun in case Bravington followed his line of sight. As Bravington assessed the correction and picked up the lamp, Alan's eyes shifted to the Hun again. He could see it quite distinctly now, the black crosses on the underside of the lower mainplane, the observer in the rear cockpit traversing with the machine-gun as the pilot began a wide turn, preparing to come on to a parallel course with the BE2.

Bravington leaned out over the obstructing lower wing and pointed the lamp in the direction of the gun battery. But before he could make the signal an Archie shell burst directly ahead; a blinding flash, a deafening bang, and a large hole appeared on the port side of the lower mainplane. Bravington was thrown back into his cockpit as Alan struggled to regain control of his machine which was behaving like a horse gone wild with fear. Alan straightened the controls, trusting her to right herself, his eye fixed anxiously on the flapping fabric around the gaping hole in the lower wing, hoping to God it would not tear along the whole length of the wing. The moment she came out of her antics and was flying straight and level, he saw Bravington's shouting face and wildly pointing hand. Of course! The Hun! In the moments of panic, Alan had forgotten all about it. Now Bravington had seen it and assumed that Alan had not. Why the hell couldn't his pilot keep his eyes open, Bravington's accusing eyes appeared to be asking. The Hun was above and behind on a parallel course and approaching, rapidly. Through the struts and bracing wires of the German machine, Alan could see the observer aiming his gun, awaiting the moment to fire. What was Alan to do? Bravington was shouting and pointing again as he hauled his Winchester from the rack. Alan knew what he was being told to do. Fly west! Head for home! That meant turning to starboard, away from the pursuing Hun. It seemed the sensible thing to do, if one didn't think too hard about it. But it was exactly what the Hun would expect them to do. He would turn and follow, maintaining his position on a parallel course, and with his height advantage and superior speed ... Alan could already feel the bullets from that menacing machine-gun ripping through his body. He gritted his teeth and made his decision. Perhaps he was making a big mistake. But he'd made enough mistakes already so one more wouldn't make any difference. On the other hand, this might be his chance to wipe his slate clean. He cut the engine, pushed the stick diagonally forward and kicked left rudder.

The Albatross dived after the spiralling BE2, the observer firing his Parabellum machine-gun. Bullets smashed the windscreen of Alan's cockpit and Bravington jolted sharply around, clutching a hand to his left shoulder and screaming out in pain. Alan centred his controls and switched on his engine, his eyes fixed on the diving Albatross, which followed suit and levelled out, several hundred feet above and still on a parallel course. Bravington, now convinced that he was flying with a madman, cursed Alan to hell as the engine cut a second time and the BE2 went spiralling again, this time to the right, directly below the Hun.

Once again, the Albatross dived after the BE2, its machinegun stuttering. Alan levelled out, then, just as the Albatross followed suit, spiralled down in the opposite direction.

'What the hell are you doing?' Bravington bawled, as the ground rose alarmingly near. 'Pull her out, for Christ's sake!'

As she glided over the hedge, Alan pulled the stick into his lap, and a few moments later he felt the comforting bumps of Mother Earth.

The German observer sighted his machine-gun on the helpless pair as they climbed desperately out of the cockpits, Alan helping Bravington, who was having difficulty with his wounded shoulder.

'I told you not to lose height, didn't I?' Bravington raged.

'I'm sorry, sir. But in the circumstances I thought it was the best thing to do.'

'Shut up and run!'

The Albatross dived as they raced for the cover of the nearby coppice. A few yards short of the trees, Bravington stumbled and fell, grimacing in agony as his wounded shoulder hit the ground. Alan, who had reached the shelter of the coppice, ran back to Bravington and flung himself to the ground beside him.

'What the hell are you doing *now*?' Bravington snarled. 'Are you determined to get yourself killed?'

The Albatross swooped low. Alan buried his face in the grass, waiting tensely for the dreaded chattering of the Parabellum. He could already feel the bullets thudding into his back. What would dying be like? Would he meet his father up there? The deafening roar began to fade and he looked up to see the German observer waving to him. In surprise and relief, he waved uncertainly back, and was smiling when he met Bravington's withering gaze.

'He must think we're a couple of idiots,' Bravington said. 'It's beneath his dignity to kill us.'

Alan came to his feet and held out a helping hand. Bravington ignored it.

'I can manage well enough,' he snapped, wondering how the hell he was going to swing the propeller with his smashed shoulder. But he had no time for further thoughts on the problem. A shot rang out and a bullet whined dangerously close. 'Get down!'

As they flung themselves to the ground for a second time, two German infantrymen appeared on the fringe of the coppice, approaching cautiously, rifles at the ready. Bravington looked furiously at Alan.

'You've brought us down on the wrong side of the lines into the bargain.'

One of the Germans barked a command and waved in the direction of the BE2.

'They're making sure we don't take off,' Bravington growled, his hating eyes fixed on the infantryman running towards their machine. 'Prisoners of bloody war. Damn and blast them! You, too! If you'd done as I told you—'

His reproving words were cut short by the crack of the revolver. The running German pitched to the ground and lay still. Bravington gaped as Alan aimed and fired again. The remaining German soldier had sunk down on to one knee, his rifle at his shoulder. The bullet caught him in the head and Bravington heard the cracking of twigs as the man heeled over, his rifle firing up at the branches above him.

'Come on!' Alan said, hauling Bravington to his feet. 'You switch on! I'll swing the prop!'

Bullets hummed and whined around them, ripping through the fabric, as they soared over the hedge. A sliced bracing wire twanged as Alan glanced back at the grey uniforms swarming from the wood.

'We've made it!' he cried, joyously. 'We've made it!'

But Bravington's expression was grim and unforgiving.

Despite his despondency, Alan put away his flying gear carefully and neatly, as always, everything in its proper place.

'You're as methodical as the Hun,' Charles grinned, ducking into the tent. 'And I hear our new Hun is not such a bad chap, after all.'

'Luckily for us,' Alan said, managing a very faint smile. 'I thought I'd gone west on my very first trip.'

'Put a foot wrong here and there, did you?'

'I made a complete mess of everything.'

Charles was philosophical. They all made a mess of it the first time over. But Alan was not to be consoled.

'We failed to knock out the Hun battery,' he said. Charles shrugged. So what? 'I thought I was being clever and brought us down on the other side of the lines.'

Charles couldn't believe his ears.

'You mean you came down on the German side?' He hooted with laughter. 'Lord! That's original, anyway. Dick Bravington didn't tell me that.'

Alan stared.

'You've been speaking to him then?'

'Yes! Just before they took him off to hospital. Matter of fact, that's why I dropped in.' He smiled at Alan's anxious face. 'Don't take it so hard. You're a blacksmith, aren't you? Where's the old iron backbone then?' And he went on about Dick Bravington. 'He's a miserable old bear but you'll have to get used to that. And that lump of shrapnel in his shoulder couldn't have helped. He asked me to give you this to have with your lunch. And he had the damned cheek to tell me that I'm no longer the best shot on the Squadron. *You* are!'

Alan stared at the bottle of wine as Charles took it from the pocket of his flying coat and tossed it on to the bed.

'So there we are then,' Charles grinned. 'Welcome to France!'